NEVER KNEEL TO A KNIGHT
Published by Edwards and Williams
Copyright © 2019 by Regina Lundgren

This is a work of fiction. Names, characters, places and incidents are either the product of the author's imagination or are used fictitiously, and any resemblance to actual persons, living or dead, business establishments, events or locales is entirely coincidental.

Printed in the USA.

Cover Design and Interior Format

© KILLION
THE
GROUP, INC.

FORTUNE'S
BRIDES
BOOK
FIVE

Never Kneel to a Knight

REGINA SCOTT

To the one and only Billy B. Bateman, a true romantic, for his encouragement and masterful storytelling, and to the Lord, who sends us unexpected companions to warm our hearts

CHAPTER ONE

London, England, June 1812

Charlotte Worthington peered out of the hired coach as it came to a stop on a narrow lane beyond Covent Garden. The houses were respectable—two rooms front and back on three levels, with an attic above for one or two servants. But the red brick façades with their white-framed windows were grimed with soot, and the stone stoop wanted sweeping.

"A knight of the realm lives here?" she asked.

Miss Thorn, seated across from her, gathered her cat Fortune close as she prepared to alight. Very likely she wasn't as nervous as Charlotte. She owned the employment agency, after all, and had arranged positions for other ladies of quality. Not a strand of her raven hair was out of place where it showed under a hat the exact shade of lavender as her eyes, and her lavender-sprigged day dress had nary a crease where it peeked out beneath her velvet spencer.

"His elevation is scheduled for the next fortnight," she explained, voice as cool and competent as her look. "This is his family home. He recently returned to it."

Perhaps he had been stationed in India or the Caribbean and was only now taking up the honor he had earned in service to the kingdom. She pictured a white-haired fellow, still fit and trim, but perhaps weary of the world.

Helping him navigate the intricacies of Society would be a worthwhile pursuit.

She certainly needed one. When she was a child, her pastimes had been dictated by her father. Ever since he had died ten years ago when she was fourteen, her life had revolved around her older brother, Frederick, Viscount Worthington. She had lived in his home, gone through the requirement of a few London Seasons, then retired to run his house and help him with his scientific endeavors. Worth had needed her help. His brilliant mind rarely stayed focused on mundane matters like food and housing. Now he was married, and Charlotte was feeling extremely *de trop*. Besides, she admired her brother's bride Lydia Villers too much to wish to confuse the servants with two mistresses in the same house. And then there was Beast.

No, she was determined not to think of Beast. As much as she admired him, he could have no place in her life. Society had rules about who the daughter and sister of a viscount could marry. As often as she'd pressed against the boundaries, she knew the folly of breaking them. She was only glad Miss Thorn and dear Fortune had been willing to find her a respectable occupation to fill her time and augment her small inheritance so that she could soon live dependent on no one.

She was to be an etiquette teacher to the newly elevated.

The title rang of purpose. Her head was high as they swept up to the door.

A blond girl of about ten answered Miss Thorn's knock, her pinafore wrinkled over her gingham dress. Wide brown eyes gazed at them, unblinking.

"We already gave," she announced, pointed chin in the air.

"How commendable," Miss Thorn said, catching the door before the girl could close it on them. "But we're here to see your brother."

"Petunia?" A woman about Charlotte's age came out of

the doorway on the right. She had warm blond hair pulled back from a round-cheeked face and the same wide brown eyes. Her day dress of saffron madras cotton betrayed a buxom figure. Petunia's older sister, most likely. Did that mean she was the daughter of Charlotte's intended pupil?

Seeing Miss Thorn and Charlotte, she hurried forward.

"Please forgive us," she said with a look to her sister. "Petunia knows she isn't to open the door to strangers." She pointed to the curving stairs behind her, and Petunia traipsed up them obediently enough. As her sister turned her back on the girl, however, Petunia stopped on the landing to watch, hands clasping the polished wood balusters.

"May I help you?" the older sister asked with a pleasant smile.

"I am Miss Thorn of the Fortune Employment Agency," Charlotte's companion said, "come to see the master of the house about a position." Fortune's tail swept back and forth as if to confirm the matter.

The young lady glanced between Miss Thorn and Charlotte, frown gathering. "I manage this household. We have no positions open, and certainly nothing for a lady."

"But you do have three young ladies and their brother who require tutoring in deportment," Miss Thorn said.

Three young ladies? All her pupil's sisters, by the sound of it. He must be unmarried, or she and Miss Thorn would have been presented to his wife.

The sister in the doorway drew herself up. "I have done my best to school my sisters in deportment. Who told you we needed assistance?"

"Why your brother himself," Miss Thorn said. "By the very act of his sudden elevation."

Fortune stood in her arms and leveled her gaze on the lady in the doorway. She blinked, Fortune blinked. She smiled.

"Your pet is lovely," she murmured, raising a hand, then

hesitating. "May I?"

"Of course," Miss Thorn said.

Slowly, gently, she stroked a hand down the silky grey fur. Fortune stretched against the touch, mouth turning up for all the world as if she was smiling. While the young lady would never be a great beauty, her answering smile spoke of great beauty within.

"If you could point me in your brother's direction," Miss Thorn said, "we can move forward."

As if mesmerized by the cat, their hostess stepped out of the doorway and let them in.

"Please wait in the sitting room, miss," she said to Charlotte with a nod to the room she'd exited. She turned for the stairs, where Petunia had disappeared now, and led Miss Thorn and Fortune upward.

Charlotte wandered into the sitting room. It was neat and clean, but well lived in. The tapestry-covered sofa had hills in places and valleys in others. The wooden arms of the two chairs opposite it were chipped, the wounds pale against the walnut. The rose-patterned wallpaper was fading to pink and mint. On the oak mantel over the hearth stood several miniatures in simple wood frames. She had just picked up one of a blond lady with a weary smile and the family's brown eyes when she heard a noise behind her.

"Oh!"

Turning, she found another young lady framed in the doorway. She looked about the age to make her debut. Unlike her sisters and the woman in the miniature, she had thick brown hair. Though she was shorter than her older sister, her figure was as curvaceous in her muslin day dress.

"Tuny said someone was here to help Matty become a knight," she said, sashaying into the room with far more confidence than Charlotte had had at that age. "But I never expected a lady."

Matty? Matthew, perhaps? A strong, proper name that touched her heart. And Tuny was clearly short for Petunia.

"I would be delighted to be of service to you and your brother," Charlotte told her. "After he's knighted, you may find yourself in higher circles."

Her eyes narrowed as if she doubted that, and Charlotte had an odd feeling they'd met before. But that was impossible. She'd never been to this part of London, and she hadn't associated with the ladies making their debuts in years.

"Higher circles?" the girl queried, the breathlessness of the question belying the skepticism in her gaze.

"She's bamming you, Daisy." Petunia squeezed past her sister into the room. "They want something from Matty, just like everyone else since his name was in the paper. Ask them why they really came to see us."

Daisy cocked her head. "Do you even know my brother?"

It was on the tip of her tongue to deny it, but something stopped her. She did know one man—one powerful, wonderful man Fate had decreed was forever beyond her reach. He had been highly featured in the papers lately. When one saved the life of the Prince Regent, one became something of a celebrity. And he tended to narrow his eyes on occasion, eyes the same shade of brown as Daisy's.

Her stomach collided with her lungs, pushing the breath from her body. Somehow, she managed to speak anyway.

"There's been a mistake," she said, hurrying past the girls. "A dreadful mistake. Miss Thorn!"

"See?" Petunia said as she and her sister followed Charlotte out into the entry hall. "I told you they were up to something."

Neither the oldest sister nor Miss Thorn answered Charlotte's call. She couldn't go through with this. She'd started down this path not only to give her brother and his bride space, but to distance herself from Matthew Bateman, otherwise known as the Beast of Birmingham. She had to stop Miss Thorn from agreeing to an alliance. Charlotte lifted her skirts and began climbing.

The soon-to-be Sir Matthew Bateman eyed the woman who'd been brought up to see him. Ivy had been highly apologetic.

"I'm terribly sorry, Matty," she'd said, shifting from foot to foot and setting the floorboards to creaking. "I know you asked us for some peace and quiet this morning. I'll just leave you to it and get back to helping Anna with the washing."

He'd thanked his sister and watched as another woman entered the room. It wasn't as if Ivy had interrupted anything important. He'd been standing in the dining room, back to the long wood table, looking out at the rear garden, which seemed to consist mostly of scraggly weeds. Well, why was he surprised? The space was barely a dozen feet square. He had never thought to hire a gardener. His sisters knew nothing about raising plants, for all their mother had named them after the things.

Besides, why did he care that it didn't look like a proper garden? Until recently, he'd been proud to earn his living, providing a home, clothing, and food for his sisters. All this lazing about was eating at his brain, what hadn't been pounded out during his boxing days.

But that wasn't why he was curt to his visitor. He'd met Miss Thorn before and knew exactly what she could do to cut up a man's peace.

"No interest," he said, crossing his arms over his chest. The coat pulled at his shoulders. Most of the second-hand coats he'd been able to purchase did. They weren't cut for a fellow of his size and activities. Very likely now that he was being awarded an hereditary knighthood he'd be expected to bespeak a proper coat from a proper tailor.

All because Prinny wanted to be generous.

"You haven't heard my proposal," Miss Thorn pointed

out.

The cat in her arms regarded him with eyes like copper pennies. He'd far rather converse with the cat than her mistress. Cats were sensible things, useful. His sisters had wanted a cat for years. Did knights own pets?

"Don't need to hear your proposal," Matthew told the woman. "We don't want any of your help."

"Ah, then you are prepared for your knighting ceremony."

His gut tightened as if prepared to deflect a blow. "It's one day. I'll survive."

"And your sisters?" she inquired politely. "How well will they survive the change?"

Matthew lowered his arms. "What do my sisters have to do with this?"

"They will find themselves on the edge of proper Society," she said primly. "With the right teacher, they could make advantageous marriages."

He'd seen enough of the upper classes to know that not all marriages were as advantageous as they seemed, but then, the aristocracy weren't the only ones to marry poorly. If he had any say in the matter, Ivy, Daisy, and Petunia would marry fine men who would love and respect them, not like the father only Ivy had mourned when he'd died as drunk as he'd lived. His sisters were smart and pretty and capable. Why shouldn't they marry a wealthy banker or even a lord like Viscount Worthington?

"So, you've brought me such a teacher, have you?" he asked the raven-haired woman in lavender before him. "Ivy seems a bit old for a governess."

"I prefer to think of my client as an etiquette teacher," she said. "A lady of breeding and taste who has herself been presented at court and survived more than one London Season."

Matthew narrowed his eyes. "If she's that much of a lady, why does she need a position?"

She ran a hand back along her pet's fur, and the cat closed

her eyes contentedly. "Her brother recently married, and she feels uncomfortable staying any longer in his home."

He could understand that. Their mother had died shortly after Tuny had been born, when Matthew was already out of the house and working as a carter for the mill, fighting boxing matches on the side to earn extra money. Their father had married again, claiming the need for someone to watch over his daughters, but their stepmother had turned Matthew's sisters, particularly Ivy, into her personal servants. It had been worse after his father had died, with the woman threatening the girls with the poorhouse if they failed to do her least bidding.

As soon as he'd won his first sizeable purse, he'd moved to London and brought them with him. Ivy had raised her sisters, taking over the running of the household when he'd begun working as a bodyguard for Lord Worthington a year ago.

"We don't have a spare bed," he warned Miss Thorn. "She'd have to stay elsewhere."

"She'll be staying with me for a time," Miss Thorn said. "I would expect a fair wage and transportation back to my establishment each day she's helping you, say Tuesdays, Thursdays, and Saturdays, for several hours."

That wouldn't be so bad. His sisters might gain the advantage, and he might learn a few things to keep from embarrassing himself when the prince awarded his knighthood. And if he did this service for a lady, he might forget the one lady he could never have.

"All right," he agreed. "She can start tomorrow."

"No!"

Matthew blinked, turning to stare at the beauty in the doorway. That thick auburn hair with its fiery highlights, the flashing grey eyes, the lithe figure, supple as a sapling. Once more his gut clenched.

"Miss…Miss Worthington?" he stammered.

She rushed into the room, so unlike her usually poised

and graceful self that he knew something terrible must have happened. He strode to meet her.

"What is it?" he demanded, taking her hands. "Is it your brother? Has there been another threatening letter?"

"No, no." She pulled away, gathering her dignity like a queenly robe. Drawing an audible breath through her nose, she raised her head and met his gaze, hers now cool, emotionless.

"There's been a mistake," she said firmly. "I'm sorry we troubled you."

Matthew glanced between her and Miss Thorn, realization dawning and bringing horror with it. "*You're* the impoverished lady I'll be helping?"

Her delicate chin hardened until he would have hesitated to face her across the boxing square. "Scarcely impoverished, sir. Nor are you the white-haired gentleman I was promised."

Miss Thorn gathered her cat closer, smile still pleasant. "I never claimed Miss Worthington was impoverished, and I certainly never commented on the color of Mr. Bateman's hair. I see no purpose in protesting, unless you can give me good reason, Miss Worthington."

She opened her mouth, closed it again, then bit her lip. Such a pretty lip too, pink and warm looking. Matthew snapped his gaze to her face. Were those tears in her eyes? What had he done that was so terrible? How could he make it up to her?

"I have worked with Mr. Bateman in the past," she said. "I do not believe continued connection to be appropriate."

Now, there was a facer. Still, what did he expect? The prince might want to honor him, but most people looking at him would see the Beast of Birmingham, a boxer so brutal he had permanently maimed a man in a fight. Though more than a year had passed, few had forgotten. He would never forget or forgive himself. He wasn't sure whether Miss Worthington knew the story. Best that she never heard it.

"I concur," he said, voice and body heavy. "It would be better if we went our separate ways."

Miss Thorn sailed for the door. "A pity. The negotiations are concluded. I have accepted your offer of employment for Miss Worthington's time. She will start tomorrow at eleven. No need to thank me. The results will speak for themselves."

CHAPTER TWO

Of course, Charlotte argued with her. All the way down the stairs and out to the waiting carriage.

"I am unaccustomed to such cowardice," Miss Thorn said as the carriage started forward. She raised her chin, spine straight. Even Fortune stared at Charlotte with reproachful eyes.

Charlotte drew in a breath. Her ability to find peace in the midst of turmoil had stood her in good stead since her parents had died and her brother had taken charge. Worth could be capricious. The best way to deal with him was with calm, reason. The approach worked well with most people. Some had accused her of being aloof, unfeeling. But cowardice? That she had never faced.

Until now.

"Forgive me," she said to the employment agency owner as the carriage moved away from Covent Garden and back toward the more fashionable Mayfair. "You must not have realized the connection when you considered this position for me. Mr. Bateman once served my brother as bodyguard. It would be inappropriate for me to serve him now."

"So you, like much of London, consider yourself above him," Miss Thorn said.

That tone was as cold as a pineapple ice at Gunter's confectionary.

"No," Charlotte protested. "Not at all. I've always

considered him a gentleman. And he's being elevated."

" "Indeed." Miss Thorn cocked her head, raven curl brushing her ear. "So why the antipathy to the fellow? Was he belligerent to you when he worked for your brother?"

"Never," Charlotte assured her. In fact, there had been moments—the brush of gazes, the touch of hands—when she'd thought she'd sensed a commonality, a mutual admiration. She refused to call it anything more.

"I assume you have some loyalty to the fellow," Miss Thorn continued.

Loyalty. What a proper word. Noble, even. That's what she must feel toward Matthew Bateman, the Beast of Birmingham—loyalty.

"Certainly," Charlotte agreed, hoping the word hadn't come out too fervently.

"Then why would you entrust this task to anyone else?" Miss Thorn demanded. "Not all etiquette teachers are kind. The *ton* certainly won't be. Can you imagine the slurs and censure Sir Matthew and his sisters will face if they enter those hallowed halls unprepared?"

She could. She had been raised to her position in Society—a lady, the daughter of a viscount, from a family known for its contributions to the world. Worth was excessively proud of their heritage. So was she. But even her impressive background hadn't stopped the gossip.

Such a shame about Charlotte Worthington—three Seasons and no husband.

Small wonder she hides away with her brother's studies.

And acts as if no heart ever beat in her breast. So sad.

Charlotte shook herself. "Society can be cruel. I can see why Sir Matthew and his sisters must be prepared for their new roles in it. But I'm still not convinced I'm the right person for this position."

"Did you or did you not master the rules of the *ton*?" Miss Thorn challenged her.

"I did," Charlotte allowed. "Though at times they felt

too confining."

"You have pursued natural philosophy, conducted your own experiments though some looked down on you for it," the employment agency owner continued. "Do you know another lady more versed in bridging the gap between purpose and polite Society?"

"No," Charlotte admitted, still conflicted. "But I would be the first to point out how wide the gap and now narrow the bridge to cross it."

As if to demonstrate that it could be done, Fortune leaped nimbly between the seats to perch beside Charlotte, then bent her head to rub it against her arm. Charlotte ran her hand along the soft fur. Funny how just looking at the cat made her shoulders come down, her breath come easier.

"Fortune thinks you are exactly the right person for this position," the cat's mistress said with a nod. "And that is good enough for me. Those girls and their brother deserve a teacher who has their best interests at heart, someone who will not take advantage of them. But if you tell me you cannot put their needs before your own, I will look for another position for you."

All her life, she'd deferred to the needs of others—her father, Worth, their studies to improve industrial practices. Was this truly any different? She'd begged Miss Thorn to find her something useful, something purposeful, some place she might make a difference. If she helped Beast and his sisters, she not only gave them better lives, she paid him back for all the times he'd helped her and her brother. And as the teacher, she would be the one in control.

"Very well," she told Miss Thorn. "I'll start tomorrow, as we agreed."

Fortune began to purr.

Charlotte had regained her composure by the time she knocked on the door of the Bateman home the next day

at eleven. Her outfit helped. She generally favored green
or grey for her clothes—elegant, but practical, and the
color complimented her auburn hair—so it hadn't been
difficult to find a grey gown with simple lines and a white
tucker and cuffs. The warm June weather allowed merely
a grey and blue patterned shawl and a straw bonnet as
accoutrements. But Petunia still ogled a moment before
letting Charlotte in.

"Matty says you're to work with us first," she said over
the shoulder strap of her pinafore as she headed for the
sitting room. "He already knows everything about being
a knight."

That his sisters thought they knew everything about
being ladies was evident the moment Charlotte walked
into the room. Daisy and Ivy were dressed in satin gowns
strewn with lace at every hem and across the bodices. The
younger sister's bright smile was nearly eclipsed by the
shockingly yellow color of her gown, while Ivy all but
disappeared inside her fiery orange version. They both sat
ramrod straight, hands folded in their laps, brittle smiles on
their pretty faces.

"Miss Worthington," Ivy said, elongating each vowel.
"How nice of you to call."

"Won't you take a seat?" Daisy added with an expansive
wave, voice as laden with exaggerated refinement.

"She means sit down," Petunia whispered to Charlotte.
"We don't have enough chairs that you could take one
away."

Charlotte gave her a smile, then went to sit on one of the
remaining chairs. Petunia took the other.

They all stared at her.

Might as well practice what she intended to preach.
"How kind of you to receive me," Charlotte said. "Lovely
weather we're having."

Daisy swiveled to glance out the window. "Looks to be
coming on rain to me."

Petunia nodded. "Best we bring in the wash."

Ivy cleared her throat, and they both sat up straight again.

"Perhaps," Charlotte ventured, leaning forward, "if you told me what you've learned so far, I can determine where I might lend a hand. That is, where I might help," she quickly clarified, before Petunia could ask which hand she meant for them to borrow.

"I have done my best to teach my sisters how to be ladies," Ivy said, nose up and gaze pointed over Charlotte's left shoulder.

Daisy leaned forward in her seat, rumpling the bow on her bosom. "Ivy showed us how we should act so no one thinks we're trollops."

"To say please when you want something and thank you when you get it," Petunia added, saving Charlotte from responding for a moment. "Wipe your mouth with a napkin, not your sleeve, and don't sneeze into your hand. The last one's the hardest. How's a body to know when she's going to sneeze?"

Oh, my. Charlotte kept her smile encouraging. "Commendable. What about dancing?"

Ivy drew herself up. "We don't hold with it."

"Especially in church," Petunia put in.

"Needlework?" Charlotte tried.

Daisy preened. "I can hem a dress faster than anyone I know."

"If you're willing to stick your toe through the stitches every time you put on the dress," Petunia jibed.

Daisy gave it up and scowled at her.

"We can all mend seams, darn socks, and attach lace," Ivy reported with a look to her sisters.

"And Ivy bakes," Petunia bragged. "Popovers and pies and cinnamon buns." She sighed happily.

Charlotte refused to let her dismay show on her face. The Bateman sisters might be highly accomplished in their circle, but they knew very little of what was required to navigate the waters of Society. She had been hired to prepare them, perhaps even to help Ivy and Daisy make advantageous matches. She had much work to do. She'd need tenacity, patience. But she'd also need resources.

And she would have to be the one to explain the situation to their no-doubt doting brother.

In the little room he'd taken as his study, Matthew paced from the door to the hearth and back again for the third time in as many minutes. He'd heard the knock at the front door. He knew who was downstairs with his sisters. Ivy and Daisy had been determined to make a good impression, wearing the one set of pretty dresses their stepmother had purchased for them. For church, she'd said, as if she meant to honor the Lord instead of herself for once. She hadn't fooled Matthew. She'd wanted the girls to outshine everyone else at the little chapel to prove how prosperous they were and to hide the fact that any money she had went to her own pleasures first.

Still, Ivy and Daisy had looked as bright as canaries as they'd waited for their teacher to arrive. With any luck, Miss Worthington would see they needed no help and leave him in peace. He noticed a book sticking out of the tall walnut bookcase on one side of the wood-wrapped hearth and hastily shoved it back into place.

He still didn't understand why she was here. Lord Worthington, her brother, had married recently and was off on his honeymoon. He'd given Matthew a holiday with the understanding that they would speak about Matthew's future when the couple returned. Matthew had originally been hired as bodyguard after Lord Worthington had begun receiving anonymous threatening notes. But that danger had been unmasked and neutralized. Was he even needed?

And was it proper for him to go on serving? Gentlemen

elevated to a hereditary knighthood generally didn't work for their supper.

Then again, neither did Miss Worthington. Her brother would provide any money she needed. Why seek a position through an employment agency?

The stairs creaked. Someone was coming up. He ran his boot over the rug to tug it into place on the hardwood floor, aimed a kick at the other armchair near the fire to settle it in place. Then he hurried to take his seat in front of the hearth, head high and proud. His voice didn't waiver as he answered the knock. "Come on, then."

Miss Worthington slipped into the room. Truly, was there a more elegant lady in London? He'd seen the princesses royal at a distance when he and a squad of pugilists had been asked to accompany the prince. Those haughty ladies didn't hold a candle to the beauty in front of him.

"Done so soon?" he asked.

She regarded him, and belatedly he remembered that a gentleman stood in the presence of a lady. He climbed to his feet. She smiled, and he felt very clever.

"For the moment," she answered him. "I wanted to ask you a few questions, so I know best how to assist your sisters."

Easy enough. He might not understand the niceties of Society, but he was the only available expert on his sisters. "Ask away."

She must have considered that an invitation, for she came to sit across from him. Matthew returned to his seat. The coal settled in the grate. If he listened closely enough, he could hear her take in a breath.

She gazed at him, grey eyes as cool as a misty morning and as mysterious. "Ivy talked about teaching her sisters," she said. "Did you lose your mother early?"

Too early, though at the time he'd wondered whether his mother had had the better of it. "She died shortly after Petunia was born. Ivy was twelve at the time."

She pressed her fingers to her lips a moment. He made himself look at the fire instead.

"How awful," she murmured. "And what a burden to put on your sister."

She didn't know the half of it. "Da remarried," he told the hearth. "Our stepmother took a fancy to Tuny, at least until she was old enough to talk back."

"Did she pass away as well?"

"Not yet, more's the pity."

She gasped, and Matthew hurried on, gaze returning to hers. "She keeps house in Birmingham. I wanted my sisters closer. What else do you need to know about them?"

"Your hopes, for one," she said as if she hadn't noticed his comment. "I'm assuming you'd like Ivy to make her debut this year, even though it's late in the Season and she's older than most. We could wait and have Daisy come out next year."

Matthew cocked his head. "Come out, like with a fancy ball?"

"Or a family party," she explained.

He straightened. "Best do it all at once. Ivy will only push Daisy forward. And Daisy won't take kindly to waiting."

She nodded. "Very well then. Once they are out, I can introduce them around. Vouchers to Almack's are probably out of the question, but I'm certain I could arrange invitations to soirees and musicales."

She was outpacing him. He'd accompanied her and her brother to a ball or two, but he'd always stayed with the coach. And he wasn't entirely sure what Almack's was or why anyone would want a voucher to it. Still, he wasn't about to let her know that.

"Very well. But I intend to approve any gentleman who wants to take my sisters driving or walking or such."

She inclined her head. "Of course. That's settled, then. What about you?"

He frowned. "Me? I'm fine."

She was watching him. "You've been told what will be expected of you at the levee, then?"

By no less than three lords, all of whom had seemed certain he'd embarrass himself even with their wise counsel. He shrugged. "More or less."

She puffed out a sigh. "Come now, Beast. You must know there are expectations for your behavior."

He could feel his frown deepening. "Like what?"

"Like introductions, for one. How do you bow to the prince?"

He rose and inclined his head.

She stood and put her hand on his shoulder. "Deeper. He is the sovereign."

"And I'm a knight," Matthew reminded her. "Or I will be soon. Don't I deserve some dignity? If you're supposed to keel over for a kingly sort, do you at least kneel to a knight?"

"Never," she said. "Your obeisance is tempered by the elevation of the person you are greeting. Knights, even the hereditary ones, are at the very bottom."

"No, that's reserved for us common folk," he said.

Either the tone or the look on his face must have said more than he'd intended, for her eyes dipped down at the corners, and she removed her hand from his shoulder. "Now, then, you and your sisters may need to brush up on Society's expectations, but you know many things I've never been taught."

"Like what?" he asked, struggling to see her as anything less than perfect.

"Like boxing," she said with certainty.

Matthew snorted. "Fat lot Society needs to know about that."

"Some know far more than they should," she informed him primly. "But my point was that you are an expert in that area. For example, how would you go about besting me?"

His brows shot up. "What? You think I fight women?"

She laughed, a warm sound that made him want to move closer, as if he'd stepped through the door of his own home for the first time in a long time. "No, of course not. But you must have a strategy. Appearing before the prince is no different. You have to know what you hope to achieve."

Matthew stuck out his lower lip. "All right. But when I fight, I mostly think about staying alive, avoiding injury."

She frowned. "All defense? No offense?"

"Well," he allowed, "I did have one particular move that served me well. I can take a punch better than most, but if a fellow was especially trying, I'd wrap him up."

"Wrap him up?"

"Yeah, like this." He reached out and wrapped his arms about her, pinning her against his chest. Her eyes were wide in surprise, but he didn't see any fear in the grey. She fit against him as if she'd been tailored just for him.

He knew he should let go. Yet everything in him demanded that he hang on, hold her close, all the days of his life, no matter the cost.

CHAPTER THREE

His eyes had green flecks in them. Charlotte felt as if she were peering into the depths of a forest. His arms held her effortlessly, protecting her, cradling her. Surely this wasn't the Beast of Birmingham.

He dropped his arms and stepped back, red climbing in his cheeks. "A lady like you has no need for such tactics. And I can't very well use them on the prince."

The prince. Of course. That's why she was standing entirely too close to Beast. Charlotte stepped back as well, surprised to find her hands trembling. "Certainly not. You are being elevated for saving His Highness' life. Wrapping him up, as you call it, would jeopardize that elevation."

He regarded her a moment as if wondering whether jeopardizing his knighthood might not be a bad idea. Then he turned away to study the fire. "Won't matter. You can't make a silk purse from a sow's ear. He may knight me, but I'll never be accepted among the nobs."

Indignance raised her head. "Then you are associating with the wrong nobs. You are a fine man, Beast. There's no reason you and your sisters can't find a circle of friends."

He glanced back at her, eyes now shadowed. "If I'm such a fine fellow, why do you call me Beast?"

Her cheeks heated. "I thought that was your boxing name, a badge of honor."

He returned to his chair. "I was called that, but it was

never an honor."

"Then I beg your pardon," Charlotte said, resuming her own seat and arranging her skirts. "I suppose I should accustom myself to calling you Sir Matthew."

He grimaced. "Why? I can't accustom myself to it."

Charlotte knit her fingers over one knee. "I wonder sometimes how the sons of the higher titles manage it. The oldest son will have his father's courtesy title for years, then suddenly be called by the main title when his father passes. Worth's friend the Duke of Wey was Lord Thalston when he was younger. And highly regarded generals collect titles like pretty girls collect suitors."

"I won't," he said. "One's too much as it is."

"You'll be marvelous," Charlotte predicted. "I will make sure of it. We can start on Thursday." She stood. When he didn't, she regarded him.

He pushed to his feet. "Am I always supposed to stand around?"

"If a lady stands, you stand," Charlotte instructed him.

He scowled. My, but the look ran in the family. "How am I supposed to know which are ladies and which are plain misses?" he demanded.

She certainly had her work cut out for her. "Allow me to be clear," Charlotte said. "If a female older than ten who is not of the serving class stands in your presence, you stand until she either leaves the room or sits."

He nodded, scowl easing. "Very well. But can I ask them to sit if they hover about too long?"

"I refuse to believe those legs tire quickly, sir," Charlotte said. Then, suddenly aware of how long and strong those legs appeared in his brown trousers, she retreated a step.

"That should be sufficient for now," she told him. "I'll be back Thursday at eleven, as agreed."

She wasn't sure whether to be glad or disappointed when he didn't argue.

Her friend Lilith, however, argued quite enough for all

concerned.

Charlotte had known Lady Lilith, now Mrs.Villers, since Lilith's brother, the Earl of Carrolton, had become friends with Worth, having attended Eton together. Lilith had been vibrant once, the most sought-after lady at any event. But something had happened, her personality leaking away until she had been reduced to a bitter shell. Charlotte blamed the disappointments on the marriage mart.

Lilith had favored BeauVillers, a man of dubious character and repute, but her late father had refused to allow her to marry him. They had been reunited earlier this year, and Lilith's brother had been willing to allow the two to wed. Now that Lilith had married her dearest love, Charlotte had every hope her friend would blossom again. Soon.

"You were not at home," Lilith complained when Mr. Cowls, Miss Thorn's elderly butler, showed her into the elegant yellow and white withdrawing room. Miss Thorn had stepped out for the moment, but Fortune glanced up from her place at the window to eye their visitor with a certain calculation.

"I no longer live with my brother," Charlotte explained. "Miss Thorn was kind enough to allow me to stay for a while."

Lilith glanced around at the curved-back sofa and brace of satin-striped chairs, the tasteful display of Wedgewood and Sevres inside the glass-fronted cabinets. Fortune hopped down from the sill to pad up to her. Lilith ignored her.

"You should have your own home," she proclaimed. "A husband. I'll see to it."

Charlotte felt as if her friend had plucked the wrong string on the harp. Lilith didn't just resemble an Amazon with her impressive height, commanding figure swathed today in sapphire and white, black hair, and strong jaw. She tended to state her opinions loudly and forcefully as well, and it was a foregone conclusion that everyone in the vicinity would agree and obey.

"I'm not seeking a husband, Lilith," Charlotte told her. As if she quite concurred, Fortune abandoned Lilith and came to wind herself around Charlotte's grey skirts.

Lilith frowned. It was not as intimidating as Matthew's scowls, but it wasn't far off. "Why not?" she demanded. "I can assure you being a wife is a tremendous blessing."

"For some," Charlotte allowed. When Lilith's frown didn't ease, Charlotte took her hand and led her to sit on the sofa beside her, mindful of Fortune close by.

"Make no mistake, dearest," Charlotte said. "I'm so glad you are happy with your choice. But I'm not convinced I'd be as happy married."

"Few are," Lilith said with a contented sigh.

Fortune hopped up between them and glanced back and forth, as if considering which lap to possess first. Lilith hitched away from her. Fortune promptly pounced into her lap. Lilith recoiled.

Charlotte leaned across, picked up Fortune, and deposited her in her own lap. The grey cat pouted.

Lilith composed herself. "But even if you cannot dream of reaching my level of happiness in marriage, I can think of any number of gentlemen who might be good partners for you. Didn't I hear you were fond of Mr. Curtis last Season?"

Charlotte flinched at the fellow's name, and Fortune's ears twitched as if she didn't much like it either. "A momentary aberration," Charlotte assured her friend, running a hand down Fortune's back. "We will not suit."

"Pity." Lilith eyed them a moment as if still considering the matter, and Charlotte willed her to offer another name rather than that of the man she'd once thought might be her perfect match before he'd proven himself a liar and cheat.

Lilith merely shook her dark head. "I'll have to give the matter more thought. Perhaps Beau might know someone."

Beauford Villers had supposedly reformed, but Charlotte had never been entirely convinced of the matter.

"No need to trouble your dear husband," she said, continuing to pet Fortune, who cuddled closer. "I'm firmly on the shelf and never happier about the fact. In fact, I've found a new calling."

Lilith's smile was resigned. "Please tell me you aren't going to continue with natural philosophy. It simply isn't done."

"I did quite well the last few years," Charlotte said, hand stilling. "But no, I don't intend to continue. Thanks to Miss Thorn, I'm assisting those new to the peerage to acclimate themselves."

Lilith stared at her. "You're a chaperone?"

"Chaperone, advisor, something along those lines," Charlotte said with a wave of her hand. Fortune watched her fingers with interest. "My first assignment is Mr. Bateman, who saved the prince's life."

Lilith's brows reared up like startled horses. "Mr. Bateman, the fellow who worked for you? The Beast of Birmingham? Charlotte, you must know he's a joke."

Charlotte's spine stiffened. So did Fortune's. "If he is, it is only among people of low intelligence and lower character."

The pink in her friend's high cheeks suggested to which camp she and her husband belonged.

"Beau and I don't hold with people advancing themselves," she said, proving Charlotte's suspicions. "There is an order to the world, and all are more content when we strive to maintain it."

"Intriguing point of view," Charlotte said, fire building inside. "Did Beau think of it before or after he married into the aristocracy?"

Fortune rose and stalked up to Lilith. This time, her friend put out a hand, but more to stop the cat then to welcome her, Charlotte thought.

"That is hardly the same thing," Lilith protested. "The Villers's family is well known on the *ton*, welcome in all the best houses."

"And Mr. Bateman is admired by the Prince Regent," Charlotte countered.

Lilith patted Fortune on the head. The cat jumped down and stalked off, tail in the air and a glance of disdain over her shoulder.

"Let us not quarrel," Lilith said, watching Fortune. "I suspect you will grow weary of this pastime, just as you did those silly experiments of your brother's. When you come to your senses, I will be delighted to find you the perfect husband."

Charlotte merely offered her a polite smile. She had come to her senses sometime ago and realized she was too independent for marriage. Nothing Lilith said could change that.

Matthew was glad for a break on Wednesday from Charlotte's distracting presence. He left off the tight coat and dressed in his more comfortable loose trousers, cambric shirt, and waistcoat. He didn't even bother with a coat or cravat. He spent some time in the rear yard jogging and ferrying weighted sacks from one side of the space to the other. Might as well keep up his strength. All this sitting about could drive a man to Bedlam.

Tuny, however, had other ideas about how he should spend his time.

"Are you going to fight again?" she asked when she came out into the yard to tell him Ivy was ready for tea.

Matthew dropped the sack among the weeds. "No."

Tuny crunched up her face. "Why? You were good at it, and you won a lot of money."

He had, most of which was invested in the Exchange and bringing in a sizeable quarterly income, but he didn't intend to share that with his littlest sister. "Gentlemen don't fight, Sweet Pea."

"Ladies either, I suppose," she said with a sigh.

Matthew chuckled. "Definitely not ladies. What did Ivy bake today?"

Tuny brightened. "Sugar biscuits. Come on in, then."

He stopped by the kitchen to wash his hands and face, then followed her to the sitting room at the front of the house, where his sisters liked to gather.

Daisy and Ivy were back in comfortable clothing as well, muslin day dresses with little printed flowers speckled about the soft folds. He took his spot on the largest chair, a massive upholstered thing that sagged when he sat but nevertheless fit his frame. Daisy and Ivy were already on the sofa, the light from the windows streaming past them as Ivy took up the chipped rose-patterned teapot and poured for them all.

"I like her," Tuny announced when they'd had a few sips and one of Ivy's biscuits.

"Who?" Daisy asked from her spot beside Ivy on the sofa.

"Miss Worthington," Tuny said.

She wasn't the only one. Matthew grabbed the teapot and poured himself another cup of the thick brew, trying not to remember the feel of Charlotte in his arms yesterday.

"I don't," Daisy said, shifting on the rose-patterned upholstery and wrinkling her muslin gown in the process. "She'll have all sorts of rules. You wait and see."

Funny. Tuny was generally the skeptic in the house.

"Rules aren't so bad," Ivy mused, hands cradling her cup as if she relished the warmth. "They keep us safe. They help us build character."

Daisy tossed her head. "Perhaps I don't need more character."

"Perhaps we could all do with a bit of polish," Matthew told them.

"Not you," Tuny bragged. "You're top-of-the-trees. It was in the paper."

"Don't believe everything you read," Matthew said. "I'm still the brother you know."

"And love," Ivy said with a smile. "Still, she is right, Matty. You've moved in higher circles far longer than we have. You know about all these rules."

"I've worked with Lord Worthington for a year," he countered. "That didn't prepare me to enter Society. He's a good sort, but not what you call conventional. Nobs have their own way of doing things."

"Like what?" Tuny asked, clearly fascinated.

"Well," Matthew allowed, "did you know a gentleman's supposed to stand when a lady does?"

"How'd you know which are ladies?" Tuny demanded.

Matthew slapped his knee with his free hand. "That's what I asked." The tea sloshed, and Ivy send him a look of reproach.

"What did Miss Worthington say to that?" Daisy asked.

"That any woman over the age of ten who wasn't a servant counted," Matthew explained. He leaned back to mop the spots of tea from the arm of the chair with his napkin. It took him a moment to realize that the room had fallen silent, as if they were all waiting.

Glancing up, he found Tuny on her feet, triumph gleaming in her eyes.

"What?" Matthew asked.

Tuny raised her brows and gave him a look. Just like Charlotte. Matthew popped to his feet without thought.

Tuny tipped up her chin, then sat on the chair with a smile of satisfaction.

Matthew started to sit, and Daisy popped up. He straightened.

Daisy sat. Matthew sat. Tuny stood. Matthew stood. Tuny sat, Matthew sat, and Daisy rose. Matthew glared at them all.

Ivy started laughing, and they all joined in, even Matthew. It did his heart good to hear his sisters so happy. That's what they deserved. Maybe all this business with Charlotte and the prince would bring more happiness to his family. Why go through with it otherwise?

"Oh, Matty," Ivy said as they finally resumed tea. "I almost forgot. A letter came for you." She set down her cup and went to fetch it from among the miniatures on the mantel.

"Maybe it's from the prince," Tuny ventured, watching her sister as she returned to hand the letter to Matthew.

"Not likely." He broke the seal. The first few words sent his stomach plummeting to his knees.

"Matty?" Ivy asked, straightening beside him. "What's wrong?"

"Is it Mrs. Bateman?" Daisy asked with fear in her voice.

"Has something happened to her?" Tuny asked, her own voice starting to shake.

Matthew folded the note and rose. "It's not about your stepmother or the prince, but I need to take care of the matter. I'll try to be home for supper, but if I'm not, don't wait for me."

Because it was highly likely when he returned, he wouldn't have an appetite.

CHAPTER FOUR

The gentleman's lodging house had seen better days. So had most of its occupants. The manager answered Matthew's knock.

"Good thing you came," the thin fellow intoned in a deep voice that sounded as if it echoed from the grave. "The physician says it won't be long now."

Matthew slipped a coin into his hand. "See that he has all he needs."

"I will," Mr. Oglethorp promised, stepping aside to let him into the narrow entryway. "And when he's gone, I hope you'll see fit to keep paying for the room until I find another tenant."

Matthew's gaze was on the shadowy stairs. "We can discuss that when the time comes."

Muttering to himself, the manager trudged back down the corridor. Matthew climbed the stairs as he had once a fortnight for more than a year. The wallpaper seemed a little dingier each time, the tears and scuffs more noticeable. But Cassidy refused to allow any more help than Matthew was already giving.

Out of courtesy, he rapped on the first paneled door on the right at the top of the stairs. No one called for him to enter, but he eased open the door anyway.

It was as pleasant a room as he could make it. He'd asked Ivy's advice, though his sister had thought he was considering redecorating his bedchamber. Now cheery gingham curtains hung on the single window, and a quilt with blocks of green and brown draped the iron bedstead. Paintings of horses were hung here and there, a sign that life continued outside these confining walls. The man in the bed raised his head just enough to eye his visitor.

"You came." Cassidy's head fell back onto the pillow as his breath left him in a wheeze.

Matthew moved closer to the bed. The man under the covers had once been tall and strong enough to be known as the Giant of Lancaster. Matthew had had to have the bed especially made to fit the length of him. Now Cassidy had shrunk in on himself, his skin sticking to his skull, his limbs wasting. The light of challenge in his clover green eyes was the only sign that the fighting spirit remained.

"I always come when you ask," Matthew said, sinking onto the spindle-backed chair next to the bed.

"That you do," Cassidy allowed. "You've done more than I would have done had our positions been reversed." He paused to cough into a handkerchief, adding another patch of red to the stained linen.

"I'm not sure I believe that," Matthew said.

"And that's the difference between us," Cassidy answered lowering his hand. "If I'd hurt you in that fight, I'd have gone on with my life. You haven't. I must admit I haven't minded watching you suffer."

The cough shook him again, until he curled his body around his chest.

Matthew half rose, to do what, he wasn't sure. Cassidy waved a hand at the small table near the window. A stone jug and glass stood waiting. Matthew went to pour some liquid into a glass. The color looked too dark to be water. One sniff, and he set the cup down.

Cassidy made a face as the fit passed. "So, you'll deny me that small comfort."

"You're a mean drunk," Matthew said. "Mr. Oglethorp

doesn't deserve your bile."

"And neither do you," Cassidy agreed as Matthew returned to the bedside. "That's why I asked you here. A man starts to think when he's about to meet his Maker. I may not be able to stand on my feet on this Earth, but I'd like to be able to stand before Him in Heaven. So I ask your forgiveness."

Matthew reared back. "*My* forgiveness?"

Cassidy's eyes narrowed. "You know why. I goaded you that day. I thought if I angered you, you'd make a mistake, give me an opening. Instead, I nearly died under your pounding."

Matthew dropped back onto the chair. "It does me no honor to remember."

"And I've enjoyed watching you try to make amends," Cassidy assured him, hands smoothing the covers over his chest. "But if I'm to earn my spot with the angels, I need to set you free, the rector tells me. So I forgive you as well."

"Do you?" Matthew couldn't believe it.

He barked a laugh and started coughing again. When he finished, Matthew had pity and went for the glass. Cassidy downed the contents.

"Yes, I do," the former fighter insisted, shoving the glass back at him. "It was my own fault, poking the Beast. I should have known better. Put a nice stone on my grave, and go on about your life."

If only it was that easy. Cassidy might offer forgiveness, but Matthew couldn't accept. He'd earned the name of Beast that day, and he had not yet found a way to claim another.

Charlotte arrived for her second day of teaching with a plan and a renewed determination. Her conversation with Lilith had spurred both. The *ton* had a strange attitude about newcomers. A small amount of originality was rarely

NEVER KNEEL TO A KNIGHT   39

tolerated, while wild eccentricity was often embraced. She had no interest in making Sir Matthew and his sisters into eccentrics, but she could do what she could to help them blend in.

"I must speak to your brother first," she told Petunia when the girl answered her knock. "Is he receiving?"

"Is he receiving what?" Petunia asked, adjusting one strap on her pinafore as she stepped aside to let Charlotte in. "We didn't know about any deliveries."

"Do you think he would be willing to talk to me now?" Charlotte clarified.

Petunia nodded. "Matty's always ready to talk, well, listen, mostly. A girl can tell him most anything. He's good that way."

Funny, but Charlotte had determined the same thing. In the last year, Beast, er Sir Matthew, had stopped his work to listen to her any number of times: when she was frustrated about something Worth wanted done to his exacting criteria, when she was trying to think through an impediment in her own studies. His quiet presence had been a steady spot in her life, particularly after all the turmoil with John Curtis. That was one of the reasons she wanted to help him now.

Petunia turned to point up the stairs. "He's in the room on the right, like last time you were here. I'll tell Ivy and Daisy you'll be along soon."

Charlotte thanked her, gathered her skirts, and started climbing.

The door was open. She left it that way for propriety's sake. He was seated by the hearth as he had been last time she'd called, but his head was sunk in his hands, his shoulders slumped.

Her plan evaporated. "Beast, Matthew, what's wrong?"

He raised his head slowly, as if the weight of it was too much, and for a moment she saw a sorrow that would have broken other men. Then he composed his face and stood.

"Miss Worthington, forgive me. I just heard an old… acquaintance passed."

Charlotte hurried forward, had to stop herself from reaching out. "I'm so sorry. Had he been ill long?"

"Too long." He grimaced. "But life is like that. No need for your concern."

He wasn't going to confide further. She should not be so disappointed. She was here to help him and his sisters acclimate themselves to their new positions, not share his woes. Yet something in her yearned to touch his cheek, murmur words of solace, hear him speak of the person whose passing had left him in such despair.

"Finished with my sisters already?" he asked.

Charlotte raised her head. "I hadn't started, actually. I had a few questions for you."

"More?" he asked with the beginnings of a frown.

"A few," she admitted.

He waved her into the opposite chair. "Happy to oblige."

He didn't look happy, and she realized with a pang that she had rarely seen him smile, not since she'd been in this house and not in the last year while he'd worked for her brother. He deserved better.

She sat and arranged her green lustring skirts as he resumed his seat.

"To begin with," she said, "I'd like to know my budget."

Now that frown fell in earnest. "I agreed to pay Miss Thorn a certain amount a week. Didn't she tell you?"

"Yes," Charlotte allowed, "but that wasn't my point. If your sisters are to enter Society, they will need new clothes, accessories. The entry hall and sitting room will need redecorating. The dining room may as well if you plan to host dinner parties. Then there's the dance master, the hiring of carriages, tickets to the theatre and opera. You must have a staff member to answer the door, so Petunia doesn't have to do it. And I haven't even assessed your needs yet."

"My needs?" The words came out in a growl, but she'd heard that sound any number of times in the last year. It always appeared when she asked him to do something he found distasteful, like pour tea when she was working or escort her on some errand when he thought her brother needed his help more.

"Do you have proper clothing to meet the prince?" she challenged. "To attend a ball?"

He snorted. "No one's going to invite me to a ball."

"You might be surprised," Charlotte said. "And you might be invited to join a gentleman's club where they do things you might find of greater interest. What you are wearing will not do."

He glanced down at the brown coat and breeches he'd worn while serving her brother, then met her gaze. "One hundred pounds."

"Each?" Charlotte verified.

His cheeks darkened. "In total. It's a princely sum. See you use it wisely."

Charlotte rose, and he stood as well. He caught on quickly—she'd give him that. "I will," she promised. "I'll draw up a plan for your approval."

"No need," he said. "I trust you. I'll have the money for you on Saturday."

Warmth pushed up. Very likely that was why her cheeks felt hot again. "Thank you, Sir Matthew. Please plan on accompanying us that day. We'll be going shopping."

"Shopping?" Meredith queried as she and Charlotte dined together that evening.

"Shopping," Charlotte confirmed with a smile from her place at Meredith's right. "The very idea of it seems to have left our good knight stunned."

Meredith smiled as well, reaching down below the drape of the damask tablecloth to touch Fortune as she passed.

Normally Fortune preferred to stalk along the table itself. Meredith tolerated it when they were alone, but, with Charlotte in residence, Fortune was confined to the floor at meals. Julian would likely have to accustom himself to her pet's presence if Meredith married him.

The thought of her beau made her smile as the footman served her some of the salmon her cook had prepared for dinner that night. She and Julian had known each other since they were children, had even pledged their hearts over a wonderful Christmas. But tragedy had parted them, and the years had passed. Only recently had they become reacquainted. She was both excited and terrified that the old feelings remained. Perhaps she would always love Julian. Did it follow, though, that they were suited to each other now?

Julian seemed to think so. In the last week, he had taken her to dine at Gunther's confectionary, ride in Hyde Park at the fashionable hour, and attend the opera. His attentions were an impressive gesture, a statement to the *ton* that he was courting her in earnest. A thrill went through her each time he clasped her hand.

They had not escaped notice. She'd seen the speculative gazes aimed their way, heard the whispers. So far, none had seemed judgmental. And at the opera, His Royal Highness had glanced across the pit from his private box and extended Julian a nod in recognition. She was moving in high circles indeed.

But she couldn't help thinking that those who flew too close to the sun were destined for a fall.

"Still," Charlotte said, "he provided a budget of one hundred pounds to outfit two young ladies and a gentleman plus redecorate the public rooms of their house, transport them to various events, and see to their household duties."

Meredith forced herself to focus on the conversation at hand. "A considerable sum for Mr. Bateman, I imagine," she said, flaking off some of the salmon even as a warm body brushed against her stockings. "But not a great deal when entering Society."

"Not a great deal at all," Charlotte agreed. She pushed her peas about her white china plate. "What do you think of economizing? I believe there are dressmakers who specialize in refitting older gowns to the current style."

There were indeed. She'd pedaled some of her gowns to make ends meet before she'd received her inheritance. Fortune leaped up onto the table. Meredith picked her up and set her back down again.

"A possibility," Meredith allowed. She nodded to her footman, who removed the salmon from the table. Fortune scampered out from under the table to follow him from the room.

"And a dance master," Charlotte added. "Might we find one still seeking clients this late in the Season, Miss Thorn?"

Meredith waved a hand. "Call me Meredith, please. We are conspirators, after all."

Charlotte nodded. "Meredith, then. And you must call me Charlotte."

Meredith inclined her head, pleased. "I believe we can find a dance master. But I have another thought to help you in your work. I support good causes. What if I match Sir Matthew's investment?"

Charlotte sat back. "You'd do that?"

She shrugged. "My dear, what good is an inheritance if not to help others? Consider the money yours."

Charlotte beamed. "Thank you, Meredith. I assure you this is an excellent cause. Miss Bateman and her sisters are dears. I know with the right training and appropriate outfits, they will be welcomed."

Meredith smiled and returned to her salmon. She of all people knew how fickle the *ton's* support could be. She could only hope that the Batemans, and she and Julian, would find a circle of friends they could rely on.

CHAPTER FIVE

Shopping, Charlotte had said, and with such enthusiasm. Matthew shuddered just thinking the word. The only time he'd shopped with a woman had been with his stepmother, and she'd made it clear his opinion held no value. He'd been invited merely to carry the many packages she would acquire, outfitting herself with his father's money while his sisters made do with clothing they'd already outgrown.

He kept reminding himself that Charlotte Worthington was in no way like Mrs. Bateman. She wouldn't demean him or his sisters.

At least, not intentionally.

She arrived promptly at eleven and ushered Ivy and Daisy into a hired coach. Tuny had been persuaded to stay with Anna, their maid of all work, with the promise that she could visit an elderly neighbor of whom she was fond.

"He has dogs," Matthew had explained to Charlotte. "Tuny likes dogs."

It was aimless chatter, which he usually abhorred, but Charlotte smiled as if he'd said something pithy, and he thought he just might survive the day. To show her that he knew his business, he'd dressed in the one black coat and breeches he owned. They'd last been worn at his father's funeral and fit him badly. But they were a better material and cut than the brown. Ivy had helped him knot a passable cravat. He fancied he looked as good as any of the gentlemen strolling down the shop-filled avenue.

The feeling lasted only until he stepped into the dressmaker's establishment.

He'd never seen such an explosion of color and texture—bolts of bright satin, dusky velvet, and soft wool. Laces and bows and ribbons. And the air. He breathed in the flowery scent and promptly sneezed. Charlotte, serene in her usual grey with an ostrich plume curled around her satin-lined bonnet, offered him a commiserating smile.

The dressmaker, a tall, thin woman, looked down her beak of a nose instead. "My customers generally leave their man outside until there are packages to be carried."

Ivy and Daisy in their muslin gowns exchanged glances as Matthew's face heated.

Charlotte eyed the shop's interior and sighed. "Such a shame. I came to outfit two young ladies for the remainder of the Season, but I cannot in good conscience invest time and effort in an establishment that does not recognize quality." She allowed her gaze to meet Matthew's. "Don't you think His Highness would concur when next you speak with him at Carlton House, Mr. Bateman?"

The dressmaker was blanching as her look veered from Charlotte to Matthew. Charlotte was giving as good as she got, the minx.

He made himself look thoughtful. "Oh, I don't know, Miss Worthington. The prince tends to be the forgiving sort. I find that admirable."

"How gracious of you, sir," the dressmaker warbled, clasping long-fingered hands before her bosom. "Truly, we are honored to have such patronage and to be of assistance to such lovely young ladies. I have just the designs to emphasize their natural beauty. Please allow me to show them to you."

"I suppose we might as well, since we're here," Charlotte said grudgingly. She ushered Ivy and Daisy to padded seats, while the owner hurried to bring out various fashion plates for them to review. Matthew had to hold back a chuckle.

Charlotte waited until his sisters were thoroughly engaged, then stepped away to take him aside.

"Thank you for your assistance and understanding," she murmured, watching the dressmaker make a cake of herself over Ivy. "I think we have things in hand now. Two doors down is a milliner's. We'll go there next." She drew a piece of paper from the beaded bag at her wrist. "Three doors down on the opposite side of the street is a tailor who is expecting you. His name is Mr. Ponsonby. He knows you are to attend the next levee. Talk to him about what you want. Not brown, and nothing overly bright."

She was so serious. Matthew couldn't help teasing her. "No gilding on the lapels? Perhaps a lily embroidered on the tails?"

She stared at him.

He started laughing. "Don't worry, Miss Worthington. I won't embarrass you or the prince. I'll see you all shortly, and I'll be glad to carry any packages you might have."

She smiled, and suddenly it was difficult to leave. He made himself turn and stride out the door.

He found the tailor's shop easily enough. Ponsonby was efficient and practical, muttering to himself as he positioned Matthew in front of a semicircle of three mirrors at the back of the shop. At least this place didn't make him sneeze. A few bolts of fabric were arranged on polished cherry shelves, and an apprentice was busy cutting out a waistcoat from a length of wine-colored striped satin.

"Will the coat be a problem?" Matthew asked as the little tailor stretched the tape across his shoulders.

In the mirror to the left of him, Matthew could see Ponsonby's eyes goggling from behind thick spectacles as he read the number on his measuring tape.

"Certainly not, sir," the grey-haired tailor said, giving himself a shake and returning to his measuring. "I had the pleasure of making a coat for the Gentleman himself. His reach is just shorter than yours."

He would not preen to have longer arms than Gentleman Jackson, the Emperor of Pugilism. The fellow could still beat him in a fight, even more than a decade after Jackson's last championship match.

The bell on the shop door tinkled. Ponsonby didn't stop his work. Matthew glanced over to find that another gentleman had entered the shop. He was tall, sturdily built, and dressed the way Charlotte would likely approve. A navy coat and dun trousers appeared to be the daily uniform of a gentleman. Is that what Ponsonby would create for him?

Matthew regarded the tailor in the mirror. "Not much fond of navy."

Ponsonby had moved on to his legs. "Indeed."

"And no green," Matthew said. "Makes me look bilious."

"My greens never make anyone look bilious," the tailor replied, tsking at the reading he had just taken on Matthew's left knee. What, was one bigger than the other?

A movement caught his eye. The apprentice had hurried to speak to the newcomer, but the man's gaze veered to Matthew. He held up a hand to forestall the young man's question and wandered closer. The mirrors magnified his frame, the golden glint of his swept-back hair.

"The Beast of Birmingham, isn't it?" he drawled. "Our noble prince's newest favorite."

The tailor bustled between them before Matthew could answer. "I'll be with you shortly, Lord Harding. Mr. Bateman had an appointment."

Harding. Matthew didn't know the name. No one in Lord Worthington's set, then.

His lordship nodded pleasantly enough. "Of course. But I'm certain Mr. Bateman wouldn't mind conversing while he stands under your torture."

The tailor grimaced as he returned to his work. Matthew kept his gaze on the mirror in front of him. He'd become adept at sizing men up. In the few minutes before a match, understanding his opponent could make the difference between a rich purse and a beating. Harding was an inch or two taller than he was, but his arms were shorter. His power would likely come from those long legs. He watched as Harding's blue-eyed gaze roamed over him as well—sizing him up too. Matthew widened his stance and raised his head, eyes narrowing as they met his.

Harding didn't look away. "I have fought pugilists on occasion," he said, strolling around behind Matthew as if to measure him as thoroughly as the tailor. "Friendly matches for sport. Perhaps I could convince you to join me."

Again, the tailor spoke first. "Mr. Bateman is soon to be elevated, my lord."

"So I heard," Harding said. "Pity. But nothing says we couldn't fight each other, two gentlemen among friends."

This fellow would never be his friend. Of that Matthew was certain. "Not interested," Matthew said. "In fighting or in conversation."

The tailor's eyes sparkled appreciatively.

"I could arrange a sizeable purse," Harding said as if Matthew hadn't spoken. "That should come in handy for a gentleman with rising expectations."

The tailor slung his tape around his neck and stepped back. Matthew turned from the mirror to face the lord. "What makes you think I want or need your money?"

Harding spread his hands. "My mistake. But you're making a mistake by passing up this opportunity. Think how you will endear yourself to His Royal Highness when you win."

Was that why Harding was interested? Did he hope to win and outshine Matthew in the prince's eyes? Sad goal for a man.

"The answer is still no," Matthew told him. He turned to the tailor. "Thank you, Mr. Ponsonby."

"Of course, Mr. Bateman," he said. "A pleasure. I'll send

word when I need you for a fitting."

Harding moved to block Matthew as he started for the door. "Don't you want to erase the stain of your last fight?"

His muscles tightened, but he refused to let Harding see he'd scored a hit. Cassidy was dead now. He had no way to remedy that or the pain the man had endured as his body had wasted away.

"There's nothing that can erase that stain," he said.

Harding gave him a tight-lipped smile. "I disagree. It might surprise you to know that I'm one of the few who won't berate you for your actions. Anything can happen in the fighting square. We are all savages at heart." He leaned closer. "Tell the truth: don't you long to set the beast inside you free once more?"

He shouldn't have done it then. He refused to do it now. "No," Matthew said. "Now, pray excuse me, my lord. I'm learning to be a gentleman, and I have an appointment with a lady. You wouldn't want to keep her waiting."

Harding eyed him a moment longer, then leaned back and stepped aside with an incline of his head. He said nothing more as Matthew exited the shop.

But as Matthew headed for the milliner's, he couldn't shake the feeling he hadn't seen the last of the haughty lord.

Charlotte could not help but be pleased with their progress over the next week. Clothes had been ordered and were being delivered bit by bit. New furnishings graced the sitting room, which had been stripped of its weary wallpaper and repainted a warm cream. The new maid, Betsy, had helped clean the rooms and stood ready to answer the door, black dress covered in a white apron and blond hair covered by a ribboned cap.

Meredith and her beau the solicitor Julian Mayes were to join Charlotte and the Batemans for dinner as Ivy and

Daisy's first engagement. Ivy had been concerned about the dining room, but Charlotte had seen no need to do more than polish the cherry table and harp-backed chairs in the teal-papered space.

"I take it this dinner means we are formally out," Ivy said that evening. Charlotte had found her protégé in the kitchen overseeing the last of the meal preparations. The grey-haired Anna was hurrying about from the fire to the sturdy table in the center of the room to the sink against one wall as if she couldn't decide what to do first.

"Yes," Charlotte said, taking Ivy's arm. "And that means no more serving. You are the lady of the house, Ivy."

Ivy resisted the pressure. "Mind the roast," she instructed Anna. "You know it won't cook evenly in that fire. And be sure to cut from the ends and the middle so our guests can have their choice."

Charlotte tugged, and Ivy removed her apron and allowed herself to be led from the kitchen.

"I understand what you and Matthew hope, Miss Worthington," she said, pushing her heat-limp blond hair away from her face, "but I can't just abandon my chores. My family must eat. The house must be kept clean."

"You have two serving women," Charlotte reminded her. "They should be cooking and cleaning for you."

"But I like to cook," Ivy said with a smile. "And Tuny would be so sad if I didn't bake cinnamon buns once in a while."

"Once in a while," Charlotte stressed. "I'm certain your brother would agree that you are meant for finer things."

"He likely would," Ivy said as they started up the stairs to where Meredith's maid Enid waited to help the girls dress for dinner, having finished early with her mistress. "Matty has always wanted the best for us, and he's worked hard to make sure we had it."

Charlotte saw that in how he related to his sisters. The quartet had obvious affection for each other. He'd also brought them to London, given them a home. Now he was doing what he could to give them a better life.

"Your brother is a good man," Charlotte said as they reached the chamber story.

"He is," Ivy said. "That's why I'm glad the prince will honor him. I like seeing him happy."

At moments, Charlotte wondered if Matthew's oldest sister wasn't too accommodating. "I like seeing you all happy," Charlotte assured her. "What makes you happy, Ivy?"

Ivy paused before the bedchamber door. "I'm happiest when my family is happy, Miss Worthington. It's as simple as that."

Simple was hardly the word. The Good Book advised to love one another, but loving someone and making them happy wasn't always the same thing. Charlotte had tried to make her family happy, first her father and then her brother. She'd found the task daunting at times and frustrating at others. She could not imagine attempting to please three very different people in one household.

As she and Ivy came into the room, Enid was attempting to show Betsy how to pile up Daisy's hair and curl a few tendrils around her face. Meredith's dark-haired little maid had visited earlier in the week to advise on which fans and reticules ought to go with which pelisses and shawls and how to keep gloves up properly. Ivy had soaked in the information like water on wool, but Daisy always seemed to have a contrary opinion. It was no different now.

"Where's the rouge?" she demanded as Enid stepped back.

Ivy frowned. Charlotte came farther into the room Daisy shared with Tuny and met Enid's gaze in the mirror. "Ladies generally do not use an excessive amount of cosmetics, Daisy. A healthy regimen is the best way to ensure rosy cheeks."

As Daisy's eyes narrowed, Enid leaned closer. "But if

you're having a peaked day, Miss Bateman, you can always pinch your cheeks a bit. That generally perks them right up."

Daisy squeezed her cheeks with her fingers, then turned this way and that as if to admire the effect. Charlotte drew in a breath of relief. Perhaps everything would continue to go well after all.

As if to contradict her, from downstairs came the deep bellowing bay of a hound.

CHAPTER SIX

D aisy turned to meet Ivy's gaze. "I told you this would never work."

"What was that?" Charlotte asked as the bay came again.

Ivy's look to Charlotte was apologetic. "Tuny was offered a dog."

"And Ivy agreed," Daisy complained with a roll of her eyes.

Now came cries of dismay, the crash of crockery, punctuated by yips and yaps.

"Come with me," Charlotte ordered.

They found the dining room in chaos. One end of the tablecloth had been pulled nearly to the floor, and the plate that had been set there lay in shattered pieces among the folds. Anna was defending the door to the kitchen, roasting fork in one hand like a sword. In the corner, Matthew's youngest sister sat in a puddle of gingham, arms around the neck of a massive hound.

"Return to your work, Anna," Charlotte told her. "And don't open that door again until I tell you it's safe."

With a grateful nod, Anna did as she was bid.

Charlotte approached the pair on the floor. The hound raised its wrinkled head, sniffed, and bellowed again.

"Let me," Ivy said, joining Charlotte. She knelt beside her sister. "Tuny, you promised to keep him in the yard until we talked to Matty."

"Bit late for that," Matthew said, striding into the room. Mr. Ponsonby hadn't finished his wardrobe yet, but the black coat and breeches outlined his muscular form well. He took in the situation with a quick look. "How did we acquire a bloodhound?"

"Mr. Winthrop says he's too old to be of any use," Petunia said. "I won't let him put Rufus down. He's a good dog." She hugged him tighter as if sure he would be ripped from her arms.

Matthew joined Ivy in kneeling beside her and ran a hand over the hound's black and tan coat. Beneath a wreath of folded skin, deep brown eyes turned rheumy regarded him solemnly.

Matthew rocked back on his heels. "Did Mr. Winthrop say you could bring him home, Sweet Pea?"

"Yes," Petunia said with a hitch in her voice. "So long as you agreed to keep him. I knew you would. I'll take good care of him. He won't be any bother."

Charlotte could not be so confident. Already Rufus was drooling on the floor.

Daisy made a face. "I'm not sharing a room with a hound. He brays like a donkey."

"The yard is a little small for such a big dog," Ivy ventured, look kind as she rose.

"Then I'll walk him around Covent Garden," Petunia declared.

Charlotte tried to imagine the massive creature fitting in among the flower sellers, merchants, and pedestrians thronging the area around the Covent Garden theatre. Should he catch a scent that intrigued him, if that big nose was still capable, he could flatten little Petunia in his rush to follow the trail.

Matthew stood, gaze thoughtful. "What do you think, Miss Worthington? Would a knight own such a noble hound?"

Petunia released the dog to scramble to her feet. "Oh,

please say yes, Miss Worthington."

"Please say no," Daisy muttered, twitching her new tulip pink skirts aside.

Rufus heaved himself to his feet. His back was still straight, his head as high as Charlotte's waist. He took two steps to reach her side and pressed against her as if seeking comfort or vowing protection.

Charlotte patted the wrinkled shoulder, heart melting. "I think Rufus would make a fine addition to any gentleman's household."

Petunia squealed and gave a hop. Rufus opened his mouth, turned up his chin, and howled, the deep sound echoing through the house. Ivy's eyes widened. Daisy clapped her hands over her ears.

Matthew laughed. It was by far the finest sound Charlotte had heard in a long time, the warmth and delight lifting her mouth along with her spirits. If a dog brought him such joy, she would find him a dozen.

He was more focused on the one at the moment, patting the hound's head with a smile.

"You'll need to let him out, make him a bed in my study," he told Petunia. "I won't have him on the beds or the new furniture."

"Thank you," Daisy said fervently, lowering her hands.

"And if he requires a walk, perhaps you can take him, Matty," Ivy put in. "Even in his old age, he's too big for Tuny."

Petunia bristled, but Matthew nodded. "Agreed. And he can stay with me when you're having your lessons with Miss Worthington."

Charlotte patted the dog again. "A fine plan. Perhaps you could take him out now so that we can have our dinner."

Still chuckling, Matthew led the hound out through the kitchen, earning a scold from Anna. Petunia happily agreed to take her meal with her new pet.

Charlotte was just glad the rest of the evening went

smoothly. Even Daisy seemed a bit hesitant at first when Meredith in her usual lavender—this time an evening gown with pearls studding the gold stitching on the bodice—and Mr. Mayes in a black tailcoat with satin lapels greeted them. Charlotte could imagine the solicitor was well versed in putting people in their places, with that artfully mussed red-gold hair and warm brown eyes. But he went out of his way to be charming, and Meredith was complimentary of Ivy and Daisy. Charlotte was more concerned about Matthew and was pleased to find that he and Mr. Mayes got on well, talking about politics and her brother Worth's balloon with equal ease. The second step in her plan had been accomplished.

The third step, hiring a dance master, proved more difficult than Meredith had suggested. The best were engaged for the Season, helping those making their debuts remain current on the latest dances and instructing older ladies on changes. Charlotte attempted to teach the girls herself, but with no piano, she found it hard to keep the time.

Meredith came to her aid once again, offering the use of a pianoforte standing in an otherwise empty room on the second floor of her home. Matthew brought Ivy and Daisy over for practice. With Meredith playing and Charlotte guiding, they still made it through only a few steps. Daisy kept bumping into Ivy, and Ivy kept compensating for her sister.

Charlotte threw up her hands. "There's nothing for it. We must have a dance master."

Matthew, who had been leaning against the wall, arms across his chest, dropped his hands and straightened. "Why? Can't be all that hard to learn to dance. It's just a lot of hopping about."

"Would that it were so," Charlotte informed him. "But every piece of music has a set pattern, and there are dozens of pieces, any number of which might be played at a particular ball."

"Stuff and nonsense," he grumbled. "Dancing should be about moving to the music."

Meredith trilled a chord on the piano. "Indeed, sir. Perhaps you should take over instruction."

He shook his head.

Daisy nudged Ivy, but her gaze was on her brother. "Come on, Matty. Show them how it's done."

"Are you opposed to dancing after all?" Charlotte asked, confused. "Do you know how?"

His mouth quirked. "In a way." He stepped forward. "Ivy—clap."

His sister brought her hands together in a solid drum of a beat. Daisy joined in. Matthew began tapping one foot in time, back straight, hands on his hips. Then he leaped into the air, landed on one foot, and spun.

Charlotte stared.

He was power, he was grace, he was dance personified. His feet flicked out right, left, right again. He turned in mid-air only to land and rise again. She had never seen anything like it. She couldn't look away.

He landed, brought his feet together, and bowed. "There, now. See? Not so difficult."

Ivy and Daisy applauded. Charlotte joined in. Pink crept into his cheeks.

Meredith rose from the bench. "Quite the display of manly prowess. A shame few could match it. Perhaps that's why balls are often so dreadfully dull. I will ask Mr. Cowls to renew the search for a dance master. Come along, girls. Fortune is no doubt concerned that we have left her out this afternoon. We will take tea with her."

Ivy and Daisy followed her from the room.

Matthew remained in place until Charlotte reached his side. She managed to do so with some aplomb, praying he could not hear the fluttering of her heart.

"That was impressive, sir."

He shrugged. "Something we used to do in Birmingham to pass the time. I take it that's not how you all dance."

Charlotte smiled. "No. That's certainly not how the gentlemen dance at the balls I've attended."

He tucked her arm into his. "Perhaps you're attending the wrong balls."

"Perhaps I am." She held him in place before he could lead her across the landing to the withdrawing room. "I must thank you for something else as well. You have been very patient with all this."

He raised his brows. "I was never known for patience."

"And yet, you haven't protested as we changed your house, changed your routine."

He shifted on his feet. "As long as I don't have to light on those spindle-backed chairs in the sitting room, I'll be fine."

She'd been afraid the little gilded chairs might look too fragile to him. He probably didn't much like the new cream paint with the gold etchings either.

"You needn't sit on them," she told him. "The room was designed to appeal to the ladies who will be visiting your sisters."

A frown threatened. "Haven't seen any of those yet."

"They'll come," Charlotte promised. "Gentlemen too, if I'm not mistaken. And what news of your new wardrobe?"

He tugged at his cravat. "The coat will be ready in a few days, I'm told. But I'd prefer a less restricting neckcloth. What about the Belcher?"

Charlotte reached up and righted the white muslin. "Too messy with all that pattern. And you look so handsome in a starched white cravat."

He watched her. "Do I now?"

She found herself caught in his gaze, once more unable to look away. She made herself drop her hands and step back. "Certainly. Why else would gentlemen put up with the things?"

He shrugged again. "Well, I suppose the inconvenience is worth it if it pleases the ladies."

It pleased this lady a great deal, but she would not say that aloud.

Matthew wasn't sure why he'd shown off like that in front of Charlotte and Miss Thorn. When he'd worked as a carter, he and the lads used to lark about from time to time, dancing around a bonfire to the tune of Patrick Monaghan's trusty pipe. He'd never danced in front of a lady before.

But she hadn't protested. Indeed, the look in those grey eyes had held fascination, awe. She'd called it impressive.

That was heady stuff.

The arrival of the dance master in their lives, however, put him in his place.

The sandy-haired Mr. Durham was slender and polished in his long-tailed coat, breeches buckled at the knee in gold, and stockings as white as his perfectly tied cravat. He met Matthew with a sniff of his long nose and a curl of his lip that suggested he smelled something that had been left out too long.

But he positively gushed over Ivy.

"So graceful, so demure," Matthew heard him tell Charlotte. "A gazelle on the dance floor. I predict good things for her."

He was less kind to Daisy. "You are gliding through the steps," he informed her, "not stomping grapes like an Italian farmwife."

As if to spite him, Daisy had stomped all the harder, until the floors trembled.

"Pay him no mind," Matthew had told his middle sister as they left Miss Thorn's. "We hired him, not the other way around. He ought to be worried about pleasing you."

Daisy gave his arm a hug. "Thank you, Matty. You always

know what to say to make me feel better."

He smiled as she disengaged. Ivy might be all quiet kindness, but Daisy was all brash determination. Someday, the rest of the world was going to realize that.

But he hadn't expected that recognition to come in the form of a letter.

It was Thursday, which meant Charlotte was in residence. He had joined her and his sisters in the sitting room, standing by the hearth rather than perching on the gilded chairs, while she went over shaking hands and bowing and curtseying again. He wasn't sure he was ever going to get the hang of it. Daisy didn't want to try.

"The prince can jolly well bow to me," she said with a toss of her brown curls.

Ivy and Charlotte both protested that, and in the hubbub, Matthew caught sight of Betsy in the doorway. The maid was pale, her whole body trembling as she clutched an envelope to her chest.

"Betsy." Matthew's sharp call brought quiet to the room. "What's wrong?"

She held out the note as if it weighed far more than it should. "This just came, sir, by way of a footman all dressed in green and gold."

Ivy recovered first. She crossed to their maid and accepted the envelope. Breaking the seal, she pulled out the square of vellum. Matthew could see the gold border from the hearth.

"Trouble?" he asked, hearing the growl in his voice.

Ivy shook her head, and wordlessly passed the note to Charlotte.

Charlotte scanned the page and smiled.

"No, indeed. This is very welcome news. Ivy and Daisy have been invited to a ball. We will, of course, accept." She glanced up to meet his scowl. "And I expect you to accompany us, Matthew."

He agreed, but he was a little surprised that the thought

of attending a ball made his stomach tighten more than the thought of another fight.

His sisters seemed nearly as panicked the next few days as they scurried through the house. Ivy and Daisy muttered instructions to themselves, and he caught Ivy more than once skipping about the landing as she practiced dance steps. Charlotte changed her schedule and came over every day, for longer hours, to ensure they were prepared.

"Fuss and bother," Matthew muttered as he petted the dog.

Rufus had retreated to the study, and Matthew's side, and had to be coaxed to leave either. Petunia didn't seem to mind. She brought him tidbits from the kitchen and took hold of his collar to escort him out into the yard at least once an hour. She found an old sock and knotted it for him to chew on. The damp wool hung out of his jowls and dragged on the floor when he shambled around the room.

Matthew had confirmed with their neighbor that Tuny could keep the beast.

"He can barely see," Mr. Winthrop had complained. "Doesn't hear his own name called, can't walk more than a few steps without stopping to rest. Death would be a kindness, but if you want him, he's yours."

There was no doubt that Tuny wanted him. Matthew just wasn't sure what she'd do when it came time to bid the dog farewell.

He was just glad when the night of the ball arrived so they could get it over with.

The event was being held in rented rooms off Bond Street by the Earl of Carrolton, who Matthew knew was an old friend of Lord Worthington and his sister. Charlotte came over early with her family carriage to make sure Ivy and Daisy were ready. He couldn't help admiring the way the blue gown with its white lace edging drew attention to her auburn hair, now crowned with three bobbing ostrich plumes. She might have been made of the dainty

Wedgewood pottery he'd seen in the shops. Ivy and Daisy looked rather fine as well in their white dresses, ribbons tied at their waists and flowers twined in their hair.

"Beautiful," Charlotte told them with a smile. "You won't sit out a single dance."

He couldn't help the sinking feeling as she turned her gaze his way. Her brother had always worn black when he went out in the evenings. The coat from Mr. Ponsonby hadn't arrived yet, so Matthew was once more in funeral black, though he'd added a waistcoat striped in black and blue.

"Like the bruises you inflict," the rag merchant had joked when Matthew had purchased it some time ago.

Ivy had pressed it and sewn on fancy metal buttons, which had been yanked from the original material hard enough to leave a few holes.

When Charlotte continued to stare now, he sketched a bow. "Do I pass muster as well?"

"Very nice," she said before hurriedly turning away.

He wasn't sure why he was disappointed as he escorted them to the coach.

CHAPTER SEVEN

M atthew had ridden inside the Worthington carriage many times, but Ivy glanced around in obvious awe at the gilding on the windows, and Daisy ran a gloved hand over the padded leather seats.

"Remember," Charlotte cautioned, "do not introduce yourself to a gentleman. Allow me or your brother that honor."

Daisy made a face. "Rules. I wager not all the ladies will play by them."

Charlotte glanced out the window as the coach pulled up to take its place in the queue before the hall. "Some of the women in attendance might not. The ladies will."

And there were certainly a number of ladies mounting the stairs for the rented hall that night. Charlotte had told him Lady Carrolton was holding the ball in these rooms because the earl's townhouse was too small to admit such a company. Lord Carrolton was even now renovating a larger home he'd purchased for his bride.

Still, even though it wasn't their home, Matthew felt odd walking up the sweeping staircase for the ballroom on the upper floor. Always when he'd accompanied Charlotte and Lord Worthington he'd stayed below, in the shadows. The twinkling light from the crystal chandelier seemed too bright, the voices raised in welcome too loud. He was probably going to have to hobble himself to keep from tugging at his cravat. He stuck his hand in his pocket as they edged their way along the receiving line.

Charlotte introduced them to their hosts. Matthew took one look at the earl, and his shoulders came down. Lord Carrolton was the only man he'd ever met who was both taller and bigger. And that reach! Good thing the man had never boxed, or Matthew might not have kept his undefeated record. It was easy to look admiring as he shook the fellow's hand.

Matthew found it a little more difficult to greet the countess. She was a fiery-haired Frenchwoman with a gleam in her blue eyes, as if she knew the sort of man he was inside.

"Mr. Bateman," she greeted him in an accented voice. "Such a pleasure. I have heard much about you."

He waited for the slurs—Beast, bully, lout. Why had she invited him if she found him as distasteful as the other members of the aristocracy seemed to do?

She merely turned to Ivy and Daisy. "You are proud of your brother, *non*? To save the life of the prince."

"He's always been a hero," Ivy said with a fond look his way. Daisy wiggled her shoulders just the slightest, as if she was about to pop the hooks off her new gown, she was that proud.

"Then you must save me a dance," the countess told him with a flutter of her lashes. "I would like to dance with another hero besides my own." She beamed at her husband, who gazed besottedly back.

Charlotte nudged Matthew. Right. A response was expected.

"It would be my pleasure, Lady Carrolton," Matthew said with a bow. As he straightened, Charlotte took his arm and led him into the ballroom.

He nearly stopped and gaped. Alabaster columns soared two stories above, holding up a ceiling where the host of heavens was arrayed in all its glory. Below, fine lords and

NEVER KNEEL TO A KNIGHT

ladies walked arm in arm, pausing to chat with friends and family. Somewhere across the vast sea came the scrape of a violin.

"Stop scowling," Charlotte hissed as she paused along a paneled wall. "You'll scare off partners for Ivy and Daisy."

Matthew pasted on a smile even as Charlotte opened her mother-of-pearl inlaid fan and waved it before her. Ivy and Daisy were just behind them. They stopped too with a swish of their silky white skirts.

Daisy met his gaze and giggled. "That smile's worse than your frown. Now you look as if you ate something that disagreed with you."

He raised one hand toward his neck.

"And if you ruin that fold," Charlotte said, "I will apply this fan to your knuckles."

Matthew dropped his hand. "You're a tyrant, you know that."

Charlotte waved her fan. "Know it and relish it, sir." She nodded to an older couple who were strolling past, then brightened. "Lilith!"

A dark-haired lady in a vivid blue gown was approaching. He'd never seen one like her, nearly his height and shaped like one of those Roman statues. With that strong jaw and determined look, she might have fought Napoleon.

"Charlotte," the lady intoned with an arch look to Matthew. "Yvette mentioned she'd invited you and your… acquaintances."

She made it sound as if Charlotte had plucked them out of some back alley. Daisy must have heard the tone as well, for she raised her head in challenge, and Ivy took a step closer to her as if to protect her sister.

"Yes," Charlotte said pleasantly enough. "Allow me to introduce them to you. This is Miss Bateman and Miss Daisy Bateman and their brother Mr. Bateman. Girls, Mr. Bateman, this is Mrs. Villers, sister to the earl our host and a dear friend of mine."

The warrior woman's look softened. "How fortunate you all are to have won the support of someone of Charlotte's caliber. See that you do her credit." With a nod, she sailed on.

Matthew's fists were clenched. He forced them open.

"What, are we trained dogs to sit on command?" Daisy demanded.

"We will face worse," Charlotte predicted, but her head was high. "Some will always seek to bring you down. You task is to rise above anyway."

"Well said," Matthew told her, resolving to put the earl's sister from his mind for Ivy and Daisy's sakes. "And if anyone else troubles you two, send them my way. We'll have a little chat." He cracked a knuckle.

Daisy giggled. Charlotte shook her head. Then she straightened. "Oh, look. Here come some promising fellows."

Two gentlemen were indeed approaching out of the crowd. One was tall and slender, with brown wavy hair combed back from a face that sported a neat mustache, a short beard, and a serious demeanor. As tightly as he held himself, he wouldn't have lasted two minutes in the boxing square, even if he could have convinced himself to enter. The other had curly blond hair, a cocky walk, and a ready smile. He would be the one to watch.

"Lord Kendall, Sir William," Charlotte greeted them. "How nice to see you. May I make my friends known to you?"

"The very reason we approached," Sir William, the curly-haired fellow, proclaimed.

Charlotte introduced them to Matthew and his sisters. Ivy and Daisy simpered. Sir William promptly claimed Ivy for the next set.

Though Daisy smiled in expectation, Lord Kendall turned to Charlotte. "Miss Worthington, I would be remiss if I didn't request a dance."

Daisy's face fell. Matthew rather thought he was scowling again. Of the times he'd escorted Lord Worthington and his sister to balls, this was the first time he would see Charlotte dance. And with someone else.

It was only her due. Lord Kendall obviously knew a lady when he saw one. He was smart to ask her to partner him.

But Matthew was surprised how much he didn't like it.

Meredith couldn't get used to returning to the social scene. She'd barely been considered out, taking part in family events and attending the local assemblies, before her mother had died and she'd been forced into the role of poor relation. She'd attended events with her employer, Lady Winhaven, but that lady had been determined to keep her in the background. Now that she had her own income, she was more noticeable, but less acceptable. After all, she had chosen to go into trade by starting her employment agency for women like her who had been forced to sing for their supper. And there was the scandal that she had been accused of killing the woman who had left her her fortune.

Still, she smiled at Julian as they strolled along the edge of the dance floor. If he hadn't been such friends with Lord Carrolton since their time at Eton, she might not have been invited. Then again, Lady Carrolton had once been one of her clients, and Yvette was not one to forget a friend, no matter what heights the Frenchwoman reached in Society.

"You haven't danced yet tonight," Julian commented as they circled the end of the vast room. One set was just finishing, the gentlemen bowing and the ladies curtseying to their partners. Charlotte's pupils, the Bateman sisters, had sat out rarely. A handsome swell was even now escorting the eldest back to her brother.

"Perhaps I'm merely enjoying your company," Meredith

said, watching them.

Julian must have followed her gaze. "Ah, I hadn't realized Bateman was attending."

"Just this ball before his elevation," Meredith informed him.

Julian shook his head. "If I'd only been a few yards closer."

He had been at Lord Worthington's ill-fated balloon demonstration last month when the great scarlet bag of hot air had descended on the prince. Mr. Bateman had pulled His Royal Highness away moments before the weight had landed. If it had come down on the prince, he might have been smothered before anyone could rescue him.

"Your turn for elevation will come," Meredith promised. "You are too clever and too useful for it to be otherwise."

"Perhaps," Julian said, but his gaze remained wistful.

How it fretted him. For all she thought Julian the best of men, he had been born to a respectable but utterly untitled family. Surrounded by aristocratic friends, he worked for the prestige they had been granted at birth.

"Come," Meredith said. "Let's see how Charlotte is faring."

He smiled at her. "Always thinking about your ladies."

They followed the gilded edge of the dance floor, passing determined dowagers debating décolletés, grand gentlemen grumbling in groups. One fellow stepped into their path. He was taller than Julian, his hair blond to Julian's red-gold, his face a study in planes and lines, and his coat cut close to a muscular frame.

"Mayes," he said, voice like a blast of ice. "I didn't expect to see you here."

"I do step away from my desk on occasion," Julian acknowledged, though the arm under her hand had tensed.

"Pity. I imagine there's always a client in need of your unique sort of advice and counsel." His gaze, a silvery blue as frosty as his tone, swept over Meredith. "Make me known to the lady."

She could almost hear Julian grinding his teeth a moment before he complied. "Miss Thorn, allow me to present Lord Harding."

"My lord," Meredith said, offering her hand.

"Miss Thorn." He took her fingers for the briefest of moments, then dropped them as if she'd burned him. He returned his attention to Julian. "I believe you are acquainted with the Beast of Birmingham. Were you by chance about to speak to him?"

Julian frowned, but Meredith answered. "Mr. Bateman? Certainly."

"I suggest you encourage him to accept the offer I made him," Lord Harding said, though the words were more command than request. "It would be mutually advantageous. I'll expect word tomorrow." He strode past.

"What a shame winter came early to this part of the ballroom," Meredith said, refusing to turn and look after him. "I hope he isn't one of your clients."

"He worked with my mentor," Julian said. "I've been glad to escape his notice."

Until now. The words hung in the air. At least she had had no hand in introducing them. She tried not to think about his mentor, now Sir Alexander Prentice, who was serving the king in America. He had been the one to argue against her when she had been accused of murder. If she never saw him again it would be too soon.

"I wonder what business Lord Harding has with Mr. Bateman," she mused as she and Julian continued on their way.

"I have no intention of finding out," Julian said. "He may issue edicts, but I don't bow easily. Let's greet your knight."

Charlotte's knight, Meredith amended silently. Indeed, her client had stayed close to the former pugilist all night. That Mr. Bateman appreciated the lady's presence was evident by the way he hovered at her elbow, hand reaching for hers, then falling away before touching it. Charlotte did not appear to notice, smiling as Meredith and Julian approached.

"Meredith, Julian, so good to see you again," she greeted them.

Julian shook Matthew's hand, not even flinching when the pugilist's fingers wrapped around his. "Bateman. Thank you again for a fine dinner the other night."

Matthew nodded. "Glad to have you there. But I realized I was remiss. I didn't have a chance to thank you for taking care of Mr. Curtis for us."

At the mention of Curtis, Charlotte paled and looked away. Meredith had to stop herself from reaching out. When Charlotte had first approached her about a position, Meredith had asked Mr. Cowls what he knew of the lady. Her butler had an enviable network in London and generally kept her abreast on all her clients and their situations.

It was now widely known that the natural philosopher John Curtis, who had once been the partner to Charlotte's brother in his studies, had plagiarized Lord Worthington's work. He had also been a thorn in the side for Lord Worthington and his bride Lydia, setting up a rivalry that had resulted in the ruin of their first balloon demonstration. Few knew that Curtis had been so insidious in his attempts to gain knowledge of Lord Worthington's work that he had pretended a courtship with Charlotte. Thanks to Julian's influence, the fellow was no longer welcome in scientific circles or many ballrooms.

Julian waved a hand. "Always happy to do a favor for a friend." He turned to Mr. Bateman's sisters. "Are you ladies enjoying the ball?"

Ivy smiled politely, but Meredith couldn't help noticing that no praise left her rosy lips.

Her sister was not nearly so reticent. "I am, immensely," she declared. She took a step closer to Julian. "I'd love to dance this next set. Would you oblige, Mr. Mayes?"

Meredith blinked. Charlotte frowned. Ivy's cheeks turned as rosy as her lips.

Julian smiled gallantly. "It would be my pleasure, Miss Daisy." He offered her his arm and shot Meredith a regretful smile.

Meredith shook her head as the young beauty made off with her beau. Before Charlotte could comment, Ivy was quickly claimed as well. Yvette, Countess of Carrolton, strolled up.

"And are you ready to dance, *mon cher* Monsieur Bateman?"

Charlotte's look only darkened. Mr. Bateman eyed the Frenchwoman.

"I don't dance much," he said.

Meredith intervened. "Nonsense. I have seen you dance, sir. I'm certain you'd be delighted to partner our hostess, if only to thank her for inviting you and your sisters."

It was a pointed comment, but the pugilist merely offered the countess a tight-lipped smile. "I'm sure you can find better company."

"*Mais non,*" she said, linking her arm with his and gazing up at him under her thick lashes. "Only you will do. If you will not dance, let us promenade. *Allons-y.*"

Mr. Bateman held his ground, frown gathering. It was rather impressive. Almost as impressive as the Frenchwoman's determination.

"It's all right, Matthew," Charlotte murmured. "Give me a moment to talk with Miss Thorn."

He nodded and allowed the countess to sweep him away at last.

Charlotte drew in a breath.

"I can see I assigned you quite the challenge," Meredith said, watching Matthew's dark head bend closer to the countess' fiery mane as the two conversed.

Charlotte smiled, a ghost of its usual brightness. "They are all delightful people, if still a little rough around the edges. Terribly sorry about Daisy. We haven't covered beau poaching yet."

"And here I thought her so practiced in the art," Meredith said. When Charlotte sagged, she nudged her white satin slipper with her own. "I was joking. Julian had hinted he wanted to dance earlier. It was my own fault for not taking him up on the offer."

"Next set," Charlotte promised.

"Or not," Meredith said. "Like your clients, I find it best not to stand out."

"That was calculated risk," Charlotte told her. "They are new to all this. I have been through several Seasons, and I believe you have as well. You could reign over this crowd if you wanted."

Once she'd been young and naïve enough to want just that. Society had abandoned her when her mother died. She had seen no need to return to it now that she was self-sufficient. Yet Julian's profession as a solicitor required him to associate with the rich and titled. For his sake, she would brave much.

"Perhaps I have other goals now," Meredith said, watching Julian twirl Daisy by both hands.

Charlotte must have noticed the direction of her gaze. "Worth thinks quite highly of Mr. Mayes," she said. "He is obviously well considered by the prince and others."

"For good reason," Meredith said. "He knows how to solve their problems, even the messy ones."

Charlotte's smile returned, in full force now. "What a lovely trait to have. I hope I may soon join all of London in wishing you both happy."

So did Meredith. But if Lord Harding's reception was any indication, some would never accept her and Julian. How much would that trouble her ambitious beau?

CHAPTER EIGHT

What a night. Matthew had always been proud of his sisters, but to see so many of London's finest acknowledge them brought a smile to his face. He could find no lovelier, more poised ladies in attendance.

Except one.

He glanced at Charlotte, standing beside him now as if she guarded the crown jewels. She had stayed that close ever since Lady Carrolton had returned him to the spot.

"Such a gentleman," she'd said with a flutter of her red-gold lashes. "*Au revoir, mon cher.* I hope to hear good things of you soon."

Matthew had bowed as she sauntered away.

"Interesting conversation you appeared to be having," Charlotte had said.

Her voice had held the oddest note. In another woman, he might have thought it jealousy, but that made no sense. Charlotte didn't care for him in that way, and the countess was happily married, by all accounts, to perhaps the one fellow who might lay Matthew out flat.

"She was easy to talk with," Matthew had said. "She asked a lot of questions about Ivy and Daisy, my record in the boxing square, the incident with the balloon. I'm not sure I did myself justice, but it was good practice."

Charlotte had sniffed and trained her gaze out over the dance floor.

She had danced only a little that night, preferring to encourage Ivy and Daisy instead. He hadn't danced at all.

It wasn't because he was concerned about the steps. Despite his comments to Charlotte and Miss Thorn, he'd been certain lords and ladies danced differently than a bunch of lads behind the mill. Determined not to embarrass Charlotte or his sisters, he'd been Ivy and Daisy's practice partner after they'd left the dance master. He could acquit himself well enough. But there was only one lady he wanted to partner, and she was beyond his reach.

"The last dance of the night," Charlotte said beside him now, twisting her head this way and that to see through the milling crowds. "Ivy has a partner—Lord Kendall no less. Well done. And…yes! There goes Daisy." She sighed happily as she straightened.

Out of the masses, one man strode in their direction. Harding. His golden head was down, his eyes narrowed, as if he'd sighted a target and wouldn't deviate until he struck it. Was he after a conversation with Matthew or a dance with Charlotte?

The thought of the arrogant lord touching Charlotte fired Matthew's blood. He seized her hand. "Dance with me."

"No, no," Charlotte said, resisting with surprising strength. "The correct form is 'Miss Worthington, may I have the honor of this dance?'."

"Miss-Worthington-may-I-have-the-honor-of-this-dance," Matthew rattled off, pulling her toward the line of couples.

Lord Harding drew up and watched them pass.

Charlotte positioned herself with the ladies. With a sigh of relief, Matthew aligned himself opposite her with the men. Farther down the set, Daisy shot him a grin, and Ivy smiled. He caught himself smiling back.

This dance was a lot of hand-over-hand and twirling your partner. He nearly flung the other lady in the set out of the pattern before controlling his movements.

"Such enthusiasm, sir," she said before they parted, but she seemed to be offering more of a compliment than a complaint.

He gentled himself when he took Charlotte's arm. She floated around him, effortless, weightless, like a flower petal riding the breeze. He could have dived into the grey of her eyes, floated in peace, and never come up again.

Torture. That's what this was. To have her so close, and yet, so far. The prince might have promised to elevate him into Charlotte's sphere, but Matthew feared he would never be worthy of her. His fancy new title couldn't mask the fact that he had blood on his hands.

As if she sensed his thoughts, her smile dimmed. Her gaze sought his, held it captive once more. The world faded away. In all the vast ballroom, the teeming metropolis, there was only him and Charlotte, moving through a dance, and neither could break free.

The music stopped. He released her to her spot and bowed with the gentlemen. She curtsied with the ladies. Ivy and Daisy allowed their partners to lead them off the floor. He didn't dare offer Charlotte his arm. One touch, and his resolve would break.

He really would deserve the name of Beast if he did what he wanted right now and kissed her senseless.

Charlotte could only accord the ball a success. Ivy and Daisy had been introduced to a portion of Society, and the gentlemen at least had been appreciative. The ladies had been more reticent—additional competition on the marriage mart was always viewed with a certain amount of caution. Their brother might soon be a knight, and a baronet, but the entire family was far too close to trade. And they hadn't even owned the mill where their father had worked.

The ladies, however, had been sufficiently intrigued with Matthew. She'd seen the number of looks directed his way, most admiring. Lady Carrolton might have been the only one brave enough to approach, but others had considered doing so.

And he had only danced once, with her.

Every time she remembered, her cheeks warmed. He had mastered the more courtly forms as easily as the dance he had performed for her and his sisters. He had been there to take her hand when the pattern demanded, could be counted on to swing her gently through the turns. And, for a moment, when their gazes had brushed, she'd thought she'd seen an admiration, a regard that held her as tenderly.

But then something had intruded, a darkness slipping over him, until she'd felt as if the very air in the ballroom had soured. She could not understand it. Would he confide this time, if she asked? Did she dare ask?

Perhaps it would be best to focus on the task at hand: improving Ivy and Daisy's standing on the *ton*. Gregory, Earl of Carrolton, was one of the kindest, most considerate men she'd ever met, and no one was as open-minded as his bride, Yvette. Lilith's reception had proven that others in Society would not be as welcoming. Time for step four.

"Daily constitutionals, I think," she told Ivy and Daisy the next day when she returned to the house off Covent Garden. "In Hyde Park, between three and five, when it will be at its most crowded by all the fashionable. That should help establish you as members of the *Beau Monde*."

"Bow what?" Petunia asked from her place on the sitting room carpet. She had managed to pull Rufus away from Matthew and sat with him, legs curled away from the growing puddle around his jowls.

"Good society," Charlotte translated.

Petunia nodded. "And while you take your constitutionals, I can walk Rufus."

The elderly hound raised his head from the carpet and

blinked his rheumy eyes. Much as Charlotte knew he could do with more fresh air, she wasn't sure it was wise for tiny Petunia to drag him to the park and surround him with horses, other dogs, and children.

Daisy, seated on the sofa next to Ivy, was more vocal. "I will not be seen with that creature. He'll drool on my new shoes."

"Still wouldn't make them pretty," Petunia jibed.

Daisy tossed her head. "I don't have to listen to fashion advice from an infant."

Petunia climbed to her feet, and Rufus heaved himself up as well. "Infant? Who are you calling an infant?"

"Certainly not you," Charlotte intervened. "You have proven yourself a young lady of heart and purpose."

"See?" Petunia flipped her skirts aside to sit down again, pulling Rufus with her. "Miss Worthington says I have heart."

Daisy stuck out her tongue at her.

Ivy raised her brows. "I certainly hope you don't do that with our new acquaintances."

Daisy yanked in her tongue and clamped her lips together.

"Perhaps we should review how to behave when someone calls," Charlotte said. "After last night, I expect to hear the knocker sounding."

Ivy and Daisy set to with a will, Petunia chiming in here or there. It was some time before Charlotte could slip away and speak with Matthew.

Indeed, she found her tongue stuck to the roof of her mouth as she climbed the stairs to his study. Why? She had never felt so cautious with any of the men who had shown interest during her Seasons. Most had been content with her poise, her polite demeanor, wanting only a wife who would do them credit in social circles. John Curtis had seemed more interested in what went on behind her eyes. Unfortunately, he had turned out to be a dastard of the first order. His only true interest in her had been as a conduit to discover more about her brother's research so he could claim it as his own. After that debacle, she had tucked her heart safely away.

It was harder to keep up her pretenses with Matthew. Their shared purpose—first to help Worth construct his balloon, now to launch Matthew's sisters—united them, opening the door to something more. The dance last night had only inched the door wider. She wasn't sure she was willing to walk through.

If Matthew remembered last night with equal trepidation, he gave no indication as she knocked and was bidden to enter. Instead of sitting by the hearth this time, he was squeezed before a secretary, table down and papers strewn about. A smudge of ink marred his solid chin.

"Forgive the interruption," Charlotte said.

He raised his head. "I could use the interruption. Corn futures never made a great deal of sense."

Charlotte wandered closer. "Corn futures? Are you invested in the Exchange?"

He waved a hand over the papers. "To my consternation, some days. What do you think, will silk from the Orient or sugar from Jamaica be a better investment?"

No one had ever consulted her about such matters before. Intrigued, Charlotte leaned over his shoulder, studying the cramped handwriting. He'd detailed companies, their history, their potential for growth. "Silk," she said. "I cannot like the labor practices in our Caribbean plantations. Although I understand the Adair family is more compassionate."

"Adair," he repeated, writing the name on one of the sheets. "I'll look into that." He lay down the pen and glanced up at her. "Forgive me. Did you have a question for me?"

Charlotte smiled, stepping back. "I wanted to make sure you were ready for the levee on Wednesday."

He slumped. "As ready as I'll ever be, which isn't

saying much." He blinked and jumped to his feet, nearly oversetting the chair. "See? I should have stood the moment you walked in the room. I can't even remember that!"

"There shouldn't be any women at the levee," Charlotte consoled him. "And everyone stands in the presence of the prince."

"And I'm never to show my back to the fellow, even when leaving the room," he said as if reciting from memory. "At least I ought to be able to manage that."

"You have it easy," Charlotte told him, moving to the window and twitching the curtains wider to let more light into the small room. "The Queen holds drawing rooms for her ladies. She requires that we wear wide hoop skirts from the last century, complete with trains. Try walking backward in that."

"No, thank you, though I'm sure you managed it."

"I did." Charlotte turned to him. "And you'll do well at your presentation too. And when it's reported in the *London Gazette*, everyone will know what a hero you are."

He grimaced. "I'll never be a hero. Whole lot of fuss and bother over nothing."

Charlotte raised her chin. "You forget, sir. I was there. I saw you endanger yourself to keep His Highness safe."

He snorted. "If he'd had the sense God gave a goose, he would have moved out of the way all on his own."

"A sudden change in circumstance can surprise anyone." Charlotte returned to his side. His cravat was sagging. She reached up and righted it.

"Who's going to do that when I have to meet the prince?" he murmured.

Charlotte's hands lingered on his shoulders, so broad, so firm. "You could hire a valet."

Those brown eyes were guileless. "He'd never be as pretty as you."

Once again, she felt off-kilter, as if the world was shifting around her. She wanted to move closer, feel those strong arms come around her. But that implied more than she was ready to admit. She dropped her arms and stepped back. "Well, I certainly hope not. Now, I have a question for you."

"Anything."

So quick, so sure. A shame she didn't feel nearly so certain of the situation. "The ball went well last night, but now is not the time to retreat from the field. I suggest that Ivy and Daisy start promenading in Hyde Park in the afternoon. Petunia wants to join them with Rufus. I would approve, if you lead Rufus."

He narrowed his eyes. "Will you be joining us?"

"As often as I can, yes."

He nodded. "Then I'll come."

She wasn't sure why so small a concession pleased her this much. "Thank you. Then I shall meet you at Hyde Park corner at three for our first promenade."

He bowed. And though she had strolled Hyde Park many times over the years, she could hardly wait.

So, shortly after three, Matthew found himself strolling through Hyde Park, Rufus on a leash and remaining at his side only because of a firm hand. That nose kept twitching, the great head swinging from side to side as he tried to take it all in. Matthew knew the feeling.

Hyde Park on a sunny June afternoon was a fascinating blend of color and movement. Gentlemen in top hats and ladies with flowing trains on their riding habits rode past on noble steeds. Carriages lacquered in crimson, emerald, and buttercup trundled along, stopping every few feet so that the occupants could converse with those in other gilded coaches. Ladies in frilly muslin wandered along on the arms of polished escorts in tail coats. With the hum of discussion, he couldn't hear whether the birds were chirping in the trees they passed or had hidden their heads under their wings. And any scent of the flowers along the path was masked by the perfume of the ladies admiring them.

Charlotte walked on his other side, grey gown partially covered by a green short jacket of a material that gleamed in the light sparkling through the trees. The tall velvet hat on her auburn hair only made her look more elegant. Ivy and Daisy in muslin with shawls draped about their shoulders walked behind with Tuny between them. Charlotte had approved Tuny's church dress, a pretty flowered cotton with a profusion of lace, for the outing.

He couldn't shake the feeling he wasn't supposed to be here. This strutting about felt frivolous. He'd worked since he was a lad. He had funds he should be managing, a garden to plant. Shouldn't he be doing something more purposeful than this?

Then he realized everything Charlotte did had a purpose.

Her smile remained pleasant, her step confident, but that grey gaze kept moving as they approached the Serpentine on their left.

"Miss Everard," she acknowledged a beauty with golden ringlets escaping her silk-lined bonnet. "May I make you known to my friends?"

Matthew bowed, and the ladies began chatting. He and Tuny stepped to one side. Tuny rubbed Rufus behind one of his droopy ears.

"She's very good at this," his sister whispered.

"Yes," Matthew agreed, watching as Charlotte elicited a promise from the other lady to call on his sisters soon, "she is."

"That makes five," Charlotte said with satisfaction as they resumed their stroll past the blue-grey waters. "Perhaps two more, and then we can retire for the day."

Matthew shook his head. "You make this look easy."

"It is easy," she said, twitching her skirts away from a damp spot on the golden gravel. "The *ton* is above all else opposed to effort. Like the dances, once you learn the pattern, you simply repeat it."

"The pattern?" he asked, and he felt Daisy pressing closer as if just as interested in the answer.

"Catching their eye," Charlotte explained, "then commenting on something that commits you to nothing— the weather, their equipment or adornment, their family's health. When they respond, you attempt to prolong the conversation. And when things grow more interesting, you invite them to continue the discussion at your home."

He stuck out his lower lip. "Sounds simple enough."

"It is," she insisted. "You try."

Matthew blinked. "What?"

"You try," Charlotte repeated. "Look for someone you met at Lady Carrolton's ball. That should be an easy enough connection."

Easy, she said. Matthew frowned, gaze going out over the couples and groups approaching them along the path. Most veered away from him and Rufus, and he wasn't sure the dog was to blame. No one looked the least familiar.

Except that one older lady in the purple short jacket, walking with a lady of about her age. Hadn't she been the one to compliment his dancing at the Carrolton ball?

He put himself in their path. "Good day, ladies. Lovely weather for a stroll."

The woman from the ball clutched her reticule closer, blue eyes wide. Her companion grabbed her arm and dragged her to safety.

"What did I do wrong?" Matthew demanded of Charlotte.

"Nothing," Charlotte said, gaze following the women, who were hurrying off to the right, glancing over their shoulders from time to time as if afraid Matthew would set the hound on them. "That was Lady Callish and her sister. I distinctly remember you meeting them at the Carrolton ball."

"Maybe she doesn't like dogs," Tuny ventured.

"I told you we should have left him at home," Daisy said.

Tuny threw her arms around the dog's shoulder. "It's not Rufus' fault that he's big and scary."

"No," Charlotte murmured, turning her gaze to the path ahead. "Not at all."

He wished he could convince himself she still spoke of the dog.

"Suppose I leave the conversation to you," he said to Charlotte.

She raised her chin. "Nonsense. Nothing ventured, nothing gained."

"You can do it, Matty," Ivy encouraged him.

"So you've gotten the hang of it, have you?" he asked her over his shoulder.

Ivy's smile was apologetic. "Not at all. I find it difficult to talk to strangers. Daisy's the only one who's mastered it."

Daisy shrugged. "You just have to have confidence."

"And show interest in the other person," Charlotte added. "Look, here comes a likely subject. Lord Kendall danced with both Ivy and Daisy at the ball."

Matthew stopped, and Charlotte and his sisters gathered around, Daisy brightening and Ivy fussing with the fringe on her shawl as the lord approached them.

Matthew drew himself up. "Lord Kendall. You're looking well."

The fellow paused. He must know a tailor as talented as Mr. Ponsonby, for that bottle green coat fit his slender frame. Did he spend hours tending to his mustache and beard to prevent one hair from sticking out of place? No doubt he had a valet to tie so fine a cravat.

"Mr. Bateman, Miss Worthington, Miss Bateman, Miss Daisy," he greeted them. "Good to see you again."

"I'm Petunia," Tuny said before anyone could respond. "This is Rufus."

Rufus bobbed his head and barked as if to confirm it.

A smile hovered about his lordship's mouth. "Miss Petunia and Master Rufus. A pleasure to make your acquaintance."

He was willing to acknowledge a little girl and an elderly hound. The fellow went up in Matthew's estimation. Now, what had Charlotte said about furthering the conversation?

Daisy obviously remembered. "How refreshing to see a gentleman afoot," she declared. "I find it much more enjoyable to see the sights that way, don't you, my lord?"

"I do indeed," he assured her. "I frequently walk at home."

"And where is home?" Daisy urged, smile bright.

"Surrey," he replied. "Not far from the Duke of Wey's estate."

"Ah, that is your connection with Lord and Lady Carrolton, then," Charlotte mused. "I understand that area is particularly lovely."

"I enjoy it," he said. "Perhaps that's why I generally find the park too congested at this time of the day."

Charlotte nudged Matthew. That must be his cue to say something useful.

"It's busier than I imagined," Matthew allowed. "So what brings you out?"

His smile slid away. "One must do what one can to be part of Society."

"One must also take a moment for reflection," Ivy murmured, gaze on the ground.

He nodded. "Just so, Miss Bateman. Moderation in all things, I find, is best."

Now Daisy nudged Matthew from behind. What did she want him to do? Oh, right.

"Interesting approach," Matthew said. "Perhaps you could explain further over tea some time."

Lord Kendall stepped to one side as if determined to keep his distance. "My schedule in town is challenging, but I'll see what I can do. Enjoy the park." He touched his fingers to his hat, then continued on his way.

"Well done," Charlotte said.

Matthew snorted. "He didn't set a date."

"He might have if Ivy had encouraged him," Daisy complained.

"A gentleman who requires excessive encouragement isn't worth the bother," Charlotte said as Ivy shuffled her feet. "But as for Lord Kendall, time will tell if he's interested."

And who had attracted his attention. Daisy seemed to like the fellow, and Ivy might if she could get over her shyness. But was it his sisters or Charlotte herself who had drawn the young lord to their sides?

CHAPTER NINE

Step four was progressing nicely as they neared the date for Matthew's elevation, but Charlotte had identified an impediment. Accordingly, she requested a moment of Ivy's time the day after their meeting with Lord Kendall in the park.

"I was going to Covent Garden for flowers," Ivy said with a glance toward Petunia and Daisy, who were listening avidly. "That is still permissible for a lady, is it not?"

Charlotte had driven past the teaming square between the theatre and St. Paul's but never visited. Surely it couldn't be dangerous. She agreed to accompany Ivy, and they set out, a basket over the blue cambric on Ivy's arm.

As they came around the corner into the piazza proper, Covent Garden leaped at her to pull her into its embrace. It was loud, it was bright, and its smell was overpowering. Over the scent of fresh garlic and onions, plump cooks argued with flush-faced farmers. Bright-eyed beauties shouted over each other as they held out bouquets of flowers to passersby. Lush strawberries and heady gardenias also lent their scent to the air. If some of the women loitering along the edges of the great square wore rouge and had necklines plunging far too low over their chests for this time of the day, Charlotte chose to ignore them.

"How extraordinary!" she exclaimed, taking Ivy's free arm and pulling her here to look at pearly seashells brought in from Lyme Regis, there to find dusky grapes from Somerset. "We must come here more often."

Ivy paid the seller for the lilies she'd just purchased and arranged them in her basket. "It is a lively place. But I believe you had a reason for wishing to converse privately with me?"

Charlotte managed to tear her eyes away from a particularly pretty display of farm goods and led her back down the square. "Yes, actually. You seem hesitant around Lord Kendall. Has he done something to offend you?"

Ivy's lips, the exact color of the deep pink lilies in her basket, lifted just the slightest. "I doubt Lord Kendall has it in him to be offensive."

There was something tight and controlled about the young marquess, as if he held the true man deep inside. Charlotte understood. She had cultivated a similar demeanor.

"He is friends with the earl and countess," she ventured. "And he is rather handsome."

"Definitely handsome." Ivy's tone was wistful.

"Then why not encourage him, as Daisy suggested?" Charlotte asked.

Ivy was examining a rutabaga as if it held the secret to life. "I know you and Matthew hope to find me a suitable match—"

"An excellent match," Charlotte corrected her.

That smile hovered again. "An excellent match, then. But I sometimes wonder whether I'm ready. Until we moved to London, my world was very small. This," she waved her free hand to encompass the market, "is a significant expansion. Then we attended the Carrolton ball and began promenading in the park and met those I once considered so far above me, and everything became much, much larger. I can't quite accustom myself to it."

So, it wasn't Lord Kendall. That both encouraged and dismayed Charlotte. She might be able to, with great diligence, find a more prestigious suitor than a marquess for Matthew's sister. If Ivy was uncomfortable with all of Society, that was a greater problem.

"Some find their first Season overwhelming," she allowed as Ivy purchased several rutabagas and Charlotte decided not to comment that that was rightly Anna's duty. "The second and third are more enjoyable."

Ivy glanced her way as they started back toward the house, brows up in evident concern. "How many did you endure?"

Endure? This was worse then she'd feared. "Three, but I am an aberration."

Ivy glanced at her again as the sounds of the market began to fade. "Why would you say that? I find you admirable in all ways."

Charlotte squeezed her free arm. "Thank you, Ivy. But I see the differences between me and the other ladies of my set. Most are content to marry well and continue the social whirl. That would never satisfy me. I crave purpose, order."

"So do I," Ivy said. "Is there no hope for us, then?"

Why did Matthew's face spring to mind? Helping him and his sisters was her purpose right now. Who knew what the future held?

"There is always hope," she told Ivy. "We simply have to find the right man for you. And when we do, you must try to put yourself forward."

Ivy sighed. "I will do my best, Miss Worthington, but I am happiest among my family."

Charlotte patted her arm before pulling back. "I understand. Perhaps we should work on broadening your definition of family."

Ivy's smile blossomed at last. "I have already broadened it to include you."

The summer sun could not have made Charlotte feel warmer. "Thank you, Ivy. I would be delighted if you'd call me Charlotte."

"I would be honored, Charlotte."

They returned to the house in high companionship, to find Daisy gazing out the front window. Ivy's sister hurried to the entry to meet them as they came in the door.

"What must I know?" she demanded. "I'm having a Season too, if you please. You cannot teach Ivy something and leave me out."

Charlotte pressed her fingers to her chest. "Dear me. And here I thought only Ivy was ready for the secret curtsey."

Daisy glanced between them. "Secret curtsey?"

"She's bamming you," Ivy said, pulling the basket from her arm. "Charlotte asked me aside to take me to task on my attitude. I must do better at welcoming those we meet."

Daisy's eyes narrowed. "Well, you didn't need *Charlotte* to tell you that. I could have done as well. Even Mrs. Bateman knew when to try butter sauce."

Ivy's face tightened. "I do not intend to copy any behavior from our stepmother. If you'll excuse me, I should take these to the kitchen." She swept down the corridor.

Daisy gazed after her and heaved a sigh. "There. I've put her in a pet."

"None of you particularly like your stepmother," Charlotte surmised.

"Tuny does, a bit. Mrs. Bateman favored her. Still, our stepmother does manage to take care of herself and in style."

Charlotte could not encourage envy. "And now through Matthew's efforts and valor, you have a chance to make your own mark on Society. Let's collect Petunia and work on that secret curtsey."

Daisy glanced up the stairs. "What about Matty?"

Matthew was entirely another problem, and one she wasn't ready to deal with yet. "He claims to be ready," Charlotte said. "I'd like all of you to feel so confident."

Especially Ivy.

Despite his comments to Charlotte, the day of his elevation arrived before Matthew was ready. He stood in the anteroom in Carlton House with a dozen or so other men, all in tailored coats and satin knee breeches, stockings as white as their elegantly tied cravats. A few had collars so high they could barely turn their heads, or perhaps they stared straight ahead because they too doubted they deserved to be here.

At least his coat was comfortable for a change. Mr. Ponsonby had done an excellent job fitting the black velvet to Matthew's frame. Matthew looked as if he belonged to the prince's set. He still expected one of the haughty men to approach him and tell him it had all been a mistake.

As if drawn by his thoughts, the Vice-Lord Chamberlain strode up to him. All too easy to look down that imposing nose, peer out from under those heavy black brows. Still, one hit to that jutting chin a few inches below his would take the fellow down.

What was he thinking!

"You will be presented next, sir," the Vice-Lord Chamberlain said in a precise voice, as if incising every word on stone. "Are you prepared?"

Matthew nodded.

He consulted his silver-cased pocket watch, its fobs jingling. "I don't understand why His Royal Highness insisted on doing this publicly. Many knighthoods are granted in private."

"I'd be happy to come back another time," Matthew said, hoping that tickle on his cheek wasn't sweat.

The court official tsked and snapped shut his watch. "No. We all dance to the royal whim. Take your place before the door, if you please."

Matthew walked across the thick carpet, knowing every eye was on him. He thought men walking to the gallows looked happier.

Servants in white-powdered wigs and crimson livery stood on either side of the door. They stared past him as if he wasn't there. Someone must have signaled them, however, for as one they opened the carved double doors, and Matthew stepped through.

The hall was crowded. Voices rose and fell like waves, pulsing against the massive oil paintings, the thick draperies. Somewhere he heard a violin playing, the warm sound gentle against the noise. He walked up the center carpet as he'd been instructed, past cabinet ministers in black coats with silver buttons, swords at their waists; military heroes in scarlet and gold, plumed hats in one hand; and bishops in black silk. One fellow stood head and shoulders above the others. The Earl of Carrolton offered him a smile. Matthew took in a breath.

Closer to the top of the room stood the yeoman guards, halberds gleaming. One inclined his head ever the slightest. At least two people agreed to Matthew's elevation.

So did the fellow sitting on the raised dais under the crimson canopy.

Though he had never personally led his troops into battle, His Royal Highness wore the red of a cavalry officer, golden epaulets heavy on his shoulders and medals sparkling on his broad chest. His hands clasped the gilded arms of his chair, which was upholstered in red velvet a shade deeper than his coat. The fellow certainly liked the color. Eyes gleaming, he smiled as Matthew stopped in front of him and bowed deeply.

"Matthew Bateman, Your Highness," the Vice-Lord Chamberlain intoned.

"I know who he is," the Prince Regent declared. "Everyone in my kingdom knows who he is. Is there a man in this room who says otherwise?"

Voices quieted, men stilled. Matthew waited for the outcry, the laughter. None came.

As if to make sure of it, His Highness swept his gaze over the space, then returned it to Matthew.

"On May twenty-sixth of this year," he said, voice ringing, "you courageously protected Our Royal Personage from imminent danger, saving the life of your Prince at the risk of your own. The kingdom owes you a debt of gratitude. *I* owe you a debt of gratitude."

"Your servant, Your Highness," Matthew said, bowing again.

Prince George held out one hand. "The patents, if you please."

The Vice-Lord Chamberlain's thin lips curled just the slightest as he handed a heavily decorated piece of parchment to the prince, who raised it and squinted at the words.

"George," he read, "by the Grace of God of the United Kingdom and Ireland and of our other realms and territories, Prince Regent, defender of the faith, to all lords spiritual and temporal and all our subjects whatsoever to whom these patents shall come. Know ye that we of our especial grace, certain knowledge, and direct volition do by these patents erect, appoint, and create our most trusty and much-admired Matthew Bateman to the dignity, state, and degree of a baronet."

There was more. Surprisingly more. His Royal Highness droned on for a number of minutes. Matthew heard little of it. He was a baronet. He kept expecting someone to shout against it, demand that the prince come to his senses, tell Matthew it was all a cruel joke. But it wasn't.

He was a baronet, a hereditary knight.

The prince finished, rolled up the parchment, and handed it to Matthew with a flourish. He bowed over the paper, accepted it. What, were his fingers trembling? He tightened his grip and straightened.

"What say you, my lords?" the prince demanded.

"Well done, Sir Matthew," someone called. Others

took up the cry, until the room shook with the thunder. Matthew stood, stunned, humbled. He was a baronet.

"Yes, well done," a familiar voice put in as the echo faded. From one side of the dais, Lord Harding moved out of the shadows. Unlike many of the others, his coat was a deep blue velvet, the silver buttons large and filigreed. Their gleam matched the gleam in his cold blue eyes.

"If I may, Your Highness, I have followed the Beast of Birmingham's previous career," he explained. "He was quite talented. While I applaud your generosity in elevating him, I can only find it a shame that he must abandon the boxing square."

The prince chuckled. "Can't have my knights out brawling."

"No, indeed," Harding agreed with a smirk of a smile. "But wouldn't it be interesting, Your Highness, to see your noble champion one last time, fighting in your honor?"

What was he doing? Once more Matthew felt sweat trickling down. Harding ought to know that gentlemen didn't fight, not in a square of tamped-down dirt, surrounded by half-drunk revelers. And even if the prince hadn't seen fit to elevate him, Matthew wouldn't have been interested. He'd already made that clear. He'd worked too hard on leaving that life behind.

Yet Harding had spoken to the prince, not him. Was he allowed to respond?

The prince stroked his meaty chin with two fingers. "My champion, fighting for me, eh? That would be something."

"A tremendous event, Your Highness," Harding assured him. "Spoken of in every home in the land, I should think."

Only by those who had nothing worthwhile to do with their time. Matthew clamped his lips shut to keep from saying the words aloud.

"The stuff of legends, say you?" the prince asked Harding.

"Assuredly," Harding promised.

He had to stop this, but all the rules Charlotte had

insisted upon kept him bound and gagged.

"It might be amusing," the prince allowed. He turned to Matthew. "What do you think, Sir Matthew?"

At last. "I think His Royal Highness honors me again by entertaining the idea," Matthew said. "But it would be poor recompense for your kindness if I should abuse it by embarrassing you."

He'd thought he'd demurred well. Surely Charlotte would be pleased with his wording.

The prince waved a hand. "Embarrass me? The Beast of Birmingham? Never." He glanced at Harding. "What did you have in mind, my lord?"

Harding's smile deepened. "As His Highness knows, I am somewhat a student of the square myself. I'm sure I'm no match for your champion, but I would be willing to attempt a fight, for your entertainment, of course."

The prince's mouth turned up. "I imagine it would be quite entertaining. Your company has been diverting, Harding, but I wouldn't mind seeing you taken down a peg." He raised his voice. "My lords, I have agreed to a boxing match between my loyal champion and Lord Harding. They will fight at the earliest convenience. And I have no doubt my knight will prevail."

CHAPTER TEN

"You must stop him."

Charlotte looked up in surprise as Lilith hurried into Meredith's withdrawing room. Charlotte had only managed to sit in the last few minutes, after pacing about, wondering how Matthew's elevation was going. She had promised his sisters she would come over later in the day to hear all about it, but she hadn't expected waiting to be so difficult.

Her friend had no intention of waiting either. She must not have stopped in the entry hall long enough to give Mr. Cowls her bonnet or pelisse, for the elderly butler was puffing in her wake. Good thing Meredith and Fortune were out in the garden. The cat still didn't know what to make of Lilith.

"Stop who?" Charlotte asked. "From what?"

Lilith threw herself down on the sofa beside her and waved away the butler, who went to position himself along the wall. "Sir Matthew. The Beast of Birmingham. He's to fight again."

Gossip. It had to be. Charlotte shook her head. "I can assure you he is done with boxing and has been for some time."

"And I can assure you he agreed to a fight with Lord Harding."

Lilith seemed so certain, dark eyes shining in her fervor.

Charlotte glanced at the butler. Meredith claimed he knew
things before anyone else in the metropolis. Catching her
eye, he inclined his balding head. Did that mean he knew
about the matter as well? How was that possible?

"Where did you hear this?" she asked Lilith.

Her friend knit her fingers together in the lap of her
serpentine pelisse. "Gregory was at the levee. He came to
tell me what happened the moment he returned. And of
course, I had to come tell you. You must stop him."

Charlotte pressed her fingers to her forehead, which felt
unaccountably tight suddenly. "Let me understand you. Sir
Matthew Bateman, at his elevation by the prince, agreed
to a boxing match?"

"With Lord Harding," Lilith insisted. "Oh, Charlotte,
after all you've done for these people, this is simply too
much. You must…"

"Stop him," Charlotte finished, lowering her hand. "Yes,
you said as much. But if His Royal Highness condoned it,
surely Society will not berate Sir Matthew for it."

Lilith sniffed. "His Royal Highness is no arbiter of taste.
And Lord Harding isn't received by many hostesses since
his unsavory habit of beating his servants became known."

She hadn't heard that bit of gossip. One of the worst
things about being in Society was the swirl of rumor and
inuendo.

"Make no mistake," Lilith continued. "If you cannot stop
this fight, you might as well disassociate yourself from this
family. They will only bring you down with them."

Just the thought of severing all ties to Matthew and
his sisters made her chest hurt. Growing up, with Worth
away at school, she'd felt so alone. She and her brother had
banded together after their parents had died. Being with
Matthew and his sisters was like having a family of her
own.

Surely all was not lost. Perhaps Gregory had
misunderstood. Perhaps Lilith's judgmental mind had

seized on a minor comment. Or perhaps a match between two gentlemen would be seen as no more than a novelty. She would investigate further before deciding what to do. That practice had stood her in good stead with her father and her brother, after all.

She managed to calm her friend and send her on her way, but Charlotte was once more pacing the room when Meredith and Fortune returned.

"Boxing is accepted as a sport, if a barbarous one," Meredith pointed out after Charlotte had explained what Lilith and Mr. Cowls had heard. "That Sir Matthew engaged in it once is scandalous enough. That he would continue fighting after his elevation will serve to ostracize him from a number of homes. His sisters as well, I fear."

It hurt further to hear even the unconventional Meredith repeat the sentiment. Charlotte didn't want her to be right. "But gentlemen race horses, yachts," she protested as Fortune scampered up to her.

"Gentlemen own horses," Meredith corrected her. "They seldom ride them in races. And they own yachts, but rarely do they actually set the sails."

Charlotte bent and scooped up the cat, who suffered herself to be petted. "They box regularly with Gentleman Jackson, who they appear to hold in high respect."

"And when was the last time you saw him at a soiree?" Meredith challenged.

The words were like damp wool, pressing down on her shoulders and chilling her. Fortune wiggled, and Charlotte let her down, feeling oddly alone again. "Then is all truly lost?"

"Unless you can change his mind or install his sisters so high in esteem the fight does not matter," Meredith said, watching her.

Charlotte sighed. "I'll go speak to him now. I promised to come hear how the levee went in any regard."

Meredith leaned back on the sofa as Fortune jumped up

beside her. "He should have quite a story to tell."

And Charlotte would have to make sure it was the last story, for his sake, and his sisters'.

"Congratulations!" his sisters chorused the moment Matthew stepped through the front door. They must have been watching for him from the window, because Tuny was still tugging Rufus out of the sitting room. The hound raised his head, black nostrils twitching. Then he let out a bay and ambled up to Matthew.

Matthew scratched him behind one droopy ear. "Thank you, one and all."

Ivy took his arm. "Come and tell us about it. What did the prince say?"

"What did he wear?" Daisy begged as Matthew allowed them to lead him into the room. He still hadn't accustomed himself to the pale colors and gold appointments. He always felt like he'd wandered into someone else's parlor. It didn't help that his favorite chair had been consigned to his study now. The gilded chairs barely fit his frame. He managed to perch on one across from the sofa as his sisters took places around him.

"Did they have cake?" Tuny asked, releasing Rufus so the dog could plop himself down next to Matthew's chair.

Matthew answered the easiest question first. "No cake. No food of any kind. There were about twenty men in the room, all dressed much like me. Though there was an African man, an ambassador of some sort I gathered, in a green silk robe with gold stitching all down the front."

"Oooh," Daisy enthused, eyes wide.

"And the prince gave a nice speech about me being a hero and handed me these papers." He waved the rolled parchment he still held in one fist. "We should put them somewhere safe."

Ivy nodded. "Your son will need them when he claims

the title."

His stomach felt hollow suddenly. A son. Who knew if he'd ever have one? And why did the child that appeared to his mind's eye have auburn hair and wise grey eyes?

He managed to answer his sisters' other questions before Ivy took the patents away for filing. She returned with a cake she'd baked for the celebration, Anna following with plates and cutlery. Ivy had just finished serving slices around when there was a knock at the door.

Daisy perked up immediately, as if expecting a gentleman to come calling, but Matthew recognized the voice requesting entry, even over Rufus's deep bark. He sat taller as Charlotte hurried into the room. Her feathered hat was askew, her grey skirts creased. Matthew rose.

"Ladies, Sir Matthew," she greeted, inclining her head. "I came as soon as I heard. Is it true? You're to fight?"

His sisters stared at him.

"Oh, Matty, you wouldn't," Ivy murmured, face puckering.

"You'll ruin everything!" Daisy cried.

"I'd wager a quid on you," Tuny put in.

"What was I to do?" Matthew demanded of Charlotte as her face fell as well. "Lord Harding was friendly with the prince, and His Royal Highness all but commanded me to fight. You don't refuse the prince. You taught me that."

"You don't refuse the prince," Charlotte agreed, venturing closer. "But you can attempt to dissuade him. I thought you were done fighting."

"So did I." Matthew shifted on his feet. "I'd already refused Harding once. He set it up so I couldn't refuse this time. I wish I knew his game."

"I'll see what I can learn," Charlotte promised.

Matthew stiffened. "No. I don't want you anywhere near the fellow. And that goes for you lot too."

His sisters nodded, eyes wide and worried. Charlotte looked less convinced, russet brows drawing down as if she didn't like being ordered about.

"But if he bows out, you can too," she said.

Harding wasn't going to bow out. Not after all the trouble he'd taken. It sounded as if he'd been high in the prince's esteem. Why else be standing so near His Royal Highness and be able to interject so easily into the conversation? But it appeared His Royal Highness was starting to lose interest. Small wonder Harding thought to reinstate himself by beating Matthew at his own sport.

"Perhaps," he allowed. "In the meantime, I'll have to practice."

"You practice beating up on people?" He could hear the distaste in Charlotte's cultured tone.

"You practice so you fight well," Matthew corrected her, stung. "Boxing is a sport. Your body must be fit, your mind ready. I'll speak to the Gentleman in the morning."

Daisy glanced around. "Perhaps we shouldn't be so Friday-faced. This could be for our good. Matthew was famous before. People treated us well."

"People treated us well because they were afraid to do otherwise," Ivy murmured.

That hurt too, though she was likely right. And if his renown protected his sisters, who was he to argue with it?

Charlotte's smile was wan. "I doubt many on the *ton* will fear your brother. Even the guests at Lady Carrolton's ball, who received you kindly the other night, may distance themselves once news of the fight becomes widely known."

She turned to him, eyes dipping down at the corners, as if she mourned for him and his sisters. "I wish you would reconsider, Matthew."

How could he? Gentlemen weren't the only ones who prided themselves on their honesty, their veracity. He shook his head. "I gave my word. There's nothing for it."

Charlotte drew in a breath and stepped back from him, and for a minute he thought she would wash her hands of them all. The thought stabbed him, made him want to take her hands, beg her to stay, promise anything to return the smile to her face, to have her regard him with something approaching approval.

"Very well," she said before turning to his sisters. "Have the maid fetch your shawls, girls. I'm taking you all to Gunter's to celebrate your brother's elevation. I will not allow this fight to diminish what is an otherwise laudable commendation."

His sisters hurried to comply, without so much as a glance his way. Rufus looked up at him as if expecting him to follow.

"It's not like you to give up on an argument," he said to Charlotte.

She eyed him. "Why, Sir Matthew, whatever made you think I was giving up? Find someone to take charge of Rufus, if you please. We have much work ahead of us."

CHAPTER ELEVEN

He wasn't sure of her. Charlotte could feel Matthew's gaze on her as she bundled everyone into her brother's carriage, which she'd taken the liberty of borrowing. It was a bit of a squeeze, but with Petunia between her sisters, they managed it.

Of course, that left Charlotte pressed against Matthew on the rear-facing seat. She was aware of the power of his body every time the coach shifted and she brushed against him. It was like pressing against a mountain. Very likely that mountain would fall all over Lord Harding, but the resulting avalanche of censure from the *ton* would bury him and his sisters as well. She had to find a way to stop this fight. Perhaps the sweets at Gunter's would inspire.

The famed confectionary was thronged with customers as her coach rolled into Berkeley Square. Dandies loitered outside the door, and waiters ran orders out to carriages.

"Do we have to eat in the coach?" Daisy asked, gazing out at all the fine ladies and gentlemen.

Petunia gave the seat a little bounce. "I don't mind. It's rather comfy."

"We will venture inside," Charlotte said, gathering her reticule. "Gunter's may be known for its ices, but it is also an excellent place to see and be seen. Follow me, ladies. Sir Matthew, if you would be so kind?"

He climbed out and helped his sisters down. As Charlotte's

fingers rested on his palm, she once again felt his strength, his surety. Oh, to spend a moment in those arms.

Not again! She composed her face and hoped it didn't look as red as it felt.

She chanced a glance to find that his scowl was back. Indeed, people in the carriages around them were staring.

"Smile," she hissed. "You've just received a great honor. Most people would be pleased."

He cocked a smile, looking sheepish. "Sorry. Habit. Tuny—halt."

He must have seen the girl darting toward traffic from the corner of his eyes. She pulled back with her sisters. Still more aware of the man at her side than the congested thoroughfare, Charlotte led them across the street and into the confectionary.

Inside was no less crowded, but a waiter directed them to a wrought iron table near the back of the main room. Similar tables dotted the black-and-white marble-tiled floor, while gentlemen were lined up six deep in front of the counter at the top of the room, the day's flavors and prices listed on slate behind.

Daisy and Petunia quizzed the waiter on which ices he'd recommend, then everyone placed an order.

"Apricot," Matthew mused with a look to Charlotte. "Interesting choice."

"It was my mother's favorite when I was a girl," Charlotte explained.

Petunia turned to her brother. "What was our mother's favorite?"

His look darkened. "We didn't get many ices in Birmingham."

"Mrs. Bateman did," Daisy said with a shudder. "I had to run all the way to Bull Street and back so it wouldn't melt, or I'd get a thrashing."

Petunia sighed. "It always looked so tasty."

Charlotte glanced between them, sure she had

misunderstood. "Did Mrs. Bateman never share her ices with you?"

Matthew shoved back from his chair and rose. "Not something we need to discuss. I'm taking a walk." He pushed through the crowds and out the door. Charlotte frowned after him.

"You must excuse him, Miss Worthington," Ivy said quietly. "Matthew never liked our father's second wife."

"She wasn't always bad," Petunia tempered.

Daisy rounded on her. "To you, because she liked you. You were just a baby when Da married her. She loved to coo over you, dress you in dainty things, then leave you with Ivy and me to change the dirty nappies."

Petunia sat higher, color pinking. "Not my fault."

"No," Ivy said with a look to Daisy. "Not your fault at all. Not any of our faults. I'm just glad Matthew could bring us to live with him. I'm sure Mrs. Bateman is much happier without us."

"Only if she found someone else to do all the work for her," Daisy muttered.

How horrid. Petunia had never known her mother. Matthew had said Ivy was only twelve when their mother had died, making Daisy around six. Charlotte had lost her mother when she was fourteen, and she still struggled with the loss some days. How much worse to lose a mother so young and be made to feel like servants in their own home?

Suddenly, Daisy brightened and elbowed Ivy. "Look. There's that handsome Lord Kendall."

The gentleman in question was standing in line at the counter, looking rather dapper in a navy coat and dun trousers. As if he suspected he was being watched, he turned to survey the crowds. His gaze met Charlotte's, and he smiled. With a quick word to the clerk, he made his way to their sides.

"Miss Worthington," he said, inclining his head. "Miss

Bateman, Miss Daisy, Miss Petunia, how good to see you again."

"Lord Kendall," Daisy said, batting her lashes.

"We're having ices to celebrate Matthew's elevation," Petunia announced.

Lord Kendall did not show any surprise at the impetuous interruption.

"An excellent reason to celebrate," he said.

"And what brings you to Gunter's on this fine day?" Charlotte asked him.

"I am a devotee of their apricot ice," he confessed.

"So is Miss Worthington," Petunia put in. "It was her mother's favorite."

"Then I am honored all the more," he said. He turned to Ivy. "And which is your favorite, Miss Bateman?"

Ivy kept her gaze on her gloved hands resting on the tabletop. "It's difficult to choose a favorite among so many wonderful flavors, my lord."

"Not for me," Daisy declared. "Licorice." She smacked her lips.

"I'm afraid I haven't had the pleasure," he said, but his gaze did not brush hers. "I should not delay your repast. Give my regards to your brother." He touched his fingers to his top hat and turned for the counter.

"You did it again," Daisy whispered to Ivy as he blended into the crowd. "Why won't you encourage him?"

"Why can't you remember what Charlotte taught us?" Ivy argued, cheeks reddening. "I doubt ladies make such noises with their mouths."

"If the food's as good as it is here, they do," Daisy said.

"Actually," Charlotte put in, "no part of a lady should make noise associated with food. Her lips, her teeth, her tongue, or areas further south."

Daisy rolled her eyes.

"And she doesn't do that either," Ivy admonished her.

"From the sound of it, she doesn't have much fun," Daisy

complained. "Perhaps I don't want to be such a fine lady after all."

"That," Charlotte said, "is your choice. But you do not have the right to behave so rudely that you endanger your sisters' choices."

Daisy's color was high, but she dropped her gaze. "Sorry."

Charlotte inclined her head, but Daisy's look had drifted to the counter, where Lord Kendall was accepting his ice. He turned to glance in their direction. But his gaze did not rest on Charlotte or Daisy. It lingered on Ivy.

What was it with these lords? Matthew spotted the fellow making eyes at Charlotte and his sisters the moment he returned to the shop. Lord Kendall still didn't look happy with his lot. And why not? He had power, privilege, and that coat, navy though it was, looked as if it had cost him a pretty penny. He could have his pick of the ladies. Why the long face?

Of course, anyone looking at Matthew might have asked the same question. Smile, Charlotte had told him. Easier said than done. Remembering how his stepmother had mistreated his sisters always put him in an ill humor. Harding's manipulation hadn't helped. Matthew was spoiling for a fight; he recognized the burning feeling in his gut. Better to take it out on a short, swift walk than poison someone else with his bile. He pasted on a smile and made himself return to the table just as the waiter brought the frozen treats they'd purchased.

Charlotte took a bite, mouth wiggling as she must have rolled the taste around on her tongue. The tiniest bit escaped those pink lips. It took every ounce of willpower he possessed not to reach out and brush it away. He shoved the spoon into the little bowl so hard it clinked against the crystal.

He was just thankful conversation remained on the

delight of the ice, until they returned to the carriage.

"Well, that was a disappointment," Daisy said, shifting on the bench until Tuny's shoulders squeezed together. "We didn't see anyone of consequence."

"Not true," Charlotte said, calmly tugging up the cuff of her glove. "Lord Kendall spoke kindly to us, that doyen of Society Lady Midmarsh was watching across the room with evident approval, and the dark-haired fellow we passed as we left was none other than Lord Byron."

"The fellow who wrote *Childe Harold's Pilgrimage?*" Daisy cried.

Not many hadn't heard about the dark and dangerous lord. Matthew hadn't been impressed—a rather sickly looking fellow, for all he was a devotee of the Gentleman. "You read that drivel?" he asked his sisters.

"We purchased a copy when it came out in March," Ivy explained.

"So did most people in London," Charlotte assured them. "After today, taking into account the attention you've received from the ball and the walks in Hyde Park, I think the next step is for us to schedule an at home."

Tuny frowned. "At home? We're usually at home."

"Unless we're promenading in Hyde Park," Daisy said.

"An at-home is a time a lady schedules to receive friends and acquaintances," Charlotte told them. "Covent Garden is a bit out of Mayfair, but I think we've whetted their appetites sufficiently that a few might attend. You can talk with them, enjoy their company, offer them refreshments."

"What would we offer them?" Daisy asked, glancing around. "Ivy doesn't know how to make those little cakes they served at the Carrolton ball."

"Cinnamon buns," Tuny said dreamily.

"Something better than those," Daisy insisted. "I don't see Lord Kendall going into raptures over cinnamon."

"Well, there is Matthew's cake," Ivy mused.

"That's ours," Tuny protested.

"Actually, it's Matthew's," Ivy reminded her.

Matthew waved a hand. "Feed it to whoever you like. I'll be too busy practicing to appreciate it properly."

Charlotte's mouth tightened. Had he broken some other rule he didn't know, or was she still stewing about the fight?

She put a hand on his arm to hold him in the carriage as they drew up before the house.

"Go ahead in," she told his sisters. "I'd like a word with your brother."

Tuny accepted that. So did Ivy.

Daisy cast him a snide glance. "You're in trouble now," she said before heading for the house.

"*I'm* in trouble?" he challenged Charlotte. "I thought a lady wasn't supposed to be alone with a gentleman in a closed carriage."

Charlotte raised her chin. "You and I were alone in a closed carriage for hours when we were chasing after Worth and Lydia."

"That was different," Matthew allowed. "They were stuck in a runaway balloon, so it was an emergency, and I wasn't considered a gentleman then."

Her chin came down. "You have always been a gentleman to me, Matthew."

He didn't believe her. She'd become so accustomed to having him around she didn't question his role. He knew better.

"What did you want?" he asked.

She rubbed a hand along her grey poplin skirts. "You and your sisters have spoken about Mrs. Bateman, your father's second wife. I gather she wasn't a pleasant person."

"She made my sisters into her personal servants, beat them, and threatened to send them to the poor house if they didn't perform to her satisfaction. If my father left my sisters any money, she spent it. I pray I never meet her again, for if I do, I won't be responsible for my actions."

She blanched, and he wanted to call back the words. Why had he reminded her of the Beast of Birmingham?

Something brushed his hand, hesitant, gentle. Glancing down, he saw Charlotte's fingers over his own.

"Please, Matthew," she murmured. "Be careful. I know you are not the brute people make you out to be, but others will judge you by your words and actions."

"They judge me just by my look," he said. "Anything I do reinforces their beliefs."

"Or refutes them," she insisted. "Your sisters have this opportunity to better their lives. Don't you want that for them?"

Matthew recoiled. "Of course I do. They deserve the best. But I can't help who I am, what I've done. It will always be a part of me."

"Is that what you want?" she murmured, gaze on their hands.

"Doesn't matter what I want."

"It does! It must!"

Surprised by her vehemence, he pulled away. "Charlotte, Miss Worthington…"

She shook herself, as if trying to regain her composure. When she spoke again, it was with her usual polished calm.

"You are master of your own destiny, Sir Matthew. Unfortunately, even in our enlightened times, that makes you master of your sisters' destiny as well. If you care about them as much as I suspect you do, you will find a way to call off this fight. And if you don't, I will find a way to call it off for you."

CHAPTER TWELVE

She'd shocked him. Charlotte could tell by the way his dark brows rose. She thought he might protest, even order her to desist. But he merely inclined his head and left her.

Truth be told, she was rather shocked by her behavior as well. He'd hired her to educate him and his sisters on the intricacies of Society, not to lecture him on his pastimes. Why had she taken him so thoroughly to task?

The question troubled her as she returned the coach to Worthington House and walked the short distance to Meredith's. She hadn't known she'd be working for Matthew when she'd asked the employment agency owner to find her a position, so she could say with a clear conscience that she had not intended to bring herself to his attention.

Perhaps she merely hated to see him trapped in this persona of a beast when she knew him to be the finest of men. Surely it had been righteous indignation, zeal for his sisters' future, that had made her speak the way she had.

At least he understood the stakes now. It was quite possible that he would move to rectify matters. That didn't mean she shouldn't try to do the same. She was the expert on Society, after all.

And so she sought out Lord Harding.

A lady never called on a gentleman—she must remember

to tell Daisy that—but nothing said she could not discover his haunts and put herself in a position of bumping into him there.

"Harding," Mr. Cowls mused when she broached the subject the next morning before breakfast. She had made sure to be up ahead of Meredith and Fortune, for just this opportunity to converse with the sage butler.

"Yes," Charlotte encouraged him when his gaze continued to focus on the pink medallions on the wallpaper behind her. "A viscount like my brother, I believe. From Yorkshire."

Mr. Cowl's distinguished nose twitched. "Not a fellow I would introduce to anyone I claimed a friend, Miss Worthington."

That did not sound good. Lilith had said he beat his servants. Perhaps that wasn't aimless gossip after all. "May I ask why?"

"A decided streak of cruelty," the butler said, moving at last to hold out a chair for her at the dining table. "I recall a horse having to be put down after he took out his spleen on the poor mare. He has risen to some notoriety this Season when he managed to enter the prince's circle. I do not expect him to stay there long, and I imagine he will lash out at any who he might see as taking his place."

Which would explain why he was so determined to fight Matthew. "And if one hoped to have a private word, purely to ensure the safety of another friend?" Charlotte asked, sitting on the chair he offered.

"I believe Lord Harding generally makes an appearance at White's before starting on his evening entertainments," Mr. Cowls said, scooting her up to the table. "What may I bring you for breakfast this morning, Miss Worthington?"

She'd requested eggs and eaten them, but her mind had remained on her purpose. She would make sure she was on St. James's not far from White's, at the proper time, even if it was when most ladies had long fled.

She took Enid with her. The energetic dark-haired maid, dressed in black from her bonnet to her practical shoes, had a scowl to rival Matthew's. Few of the gentlemen strolling past did more than cast Charlotte and Enid a curious glance before tipping their hats politely and hurrying on their way.

To give herself something to do, and a reason for being on the street, Charlotte stepped into Harris and Company and ordered scented shaving soap. She wanted the house to be ready for Worth when he returned, after all. She then strolled down the street toward Berry Brothers and Rudd, as if interested on seeking their advice about wine.

"Busybodies," Enid declared as they passed the bow window of White's gentlemen's club. Charlotte caught a quick glimpse of two fellows studying her before turning her face resolutely forward. Unfortunately, she and Enid had to stroll the pavement twice before she sighted the dusky green of Lord Harding's personal carriage. It pulled up before White's, and the door opened to allow him to step down.

"My lord," Charlotte said, nose in the air, as she passed. Enid sniffed disparagingly at him.

He removed his top hat and fell into step beside Charlotte. "Miss Worthington. An unexpected pleasure and an unaccountably cool reception. Have I offended you?"

Charlotte kept her gaze on the way ahead. "Deeply. I considered you a gentleman, sir, but any fellow who insists on fighting cannot belong to that celebrated status, despite an age-old title and respected family name."

"Ah, the fight." He shook his head, sunlight catching in the gold of his hair. "Forgive me, my dear, but pugilistic displays are for gentlemen. I wouldn't expect a lady to understand."

Charlotte jerked to a stop, forcing him and Enid up as well.

"Understand?" she asked, in a tone of voice Worth had

NEVER KNEEL TO A KNIGHT

once complained blew from the Arctic. "I understand, sir, that you are endangering a gentleman's newly won prestige, and with it the reputation of his three younger sisters. I understand, sir, that you endanger his life as well. Do you plan on endowing his sisters should something happen to him? Will you see the youngest raised to womanhood? Help the older two find suitable husbands?"

He held up his hands, lifting his top hat high. "Peace! I had no idea the fellow came encumbered, but it doesn't matter."

"Doesn't matter?" Charlotte sputtered.

"No," he insisted, lowering his hands. "Very likely Sir Matthew will win. Should he choose to wager on the outcome, he may come away a richer man, well able to support his new title."

A wager? Matthew risked his capital on the Exchange, but that was hardly the same as gambling on the outcome of a sporting event. Did he need money badly? His house wasn't in a fashionable area, and he had given her the smallest of budgets to see his sisters into Society. A shame His Royal Highness' generosity had extended only to Matthew's title. Sometimes when a man was given a title, an estate came with it.

"I will allow that the money truly doesn't matter," Charlotte told the viscount. "I am more concerned about your and Sir Matthew's reputations. It is widely accorded that a gentleman does not fight in public. Demanding that he do so demeans both Sir Matthew and yourself."

His smile was no doubt meant to be kind, but she found it infuriating. "As I said, these are matters for gentlemen to decide. I appreciate your concern, Miss Worthington, but I have risked much to arrange this fight, and I cannot cancel without having my honor impugned. Give my regards to Sir Matthew and his sisters." He slipped his hat back on his head and turned for his club. Enid glared after him.

Oh! Why were some men so pig-headed? Her father had

refused to see a physician, insisting that he would recover on his own. By the time her mother had changed his mind, his condition had been too far advanced for treatment. Worth had hidden away from Society after John Curtis had plagiarized his work. Only Lydia's return to Worth's life had pulled him out of his self-imposed isolation. Matthew seemed certain he had to honor his word and fight. Lord Harding was equally certain it was a matter of honor. Why wouldn't they both simply speak to the prince, convince him of another course of action? Could none of them see the damage they did?

Maddening—the lot of them! It would serve them right if she just washed her hands of the entire affair and walked away.

But she couldn't walk away. She had a duty to Ivy, Daisy, and Petunia. She owed it to them to make sure nothing happened to their brother. They had already lost mother and father.

"Shall we go home now, miss?" Enid asked, shifting on the pavement and setting her black skirts to swinging.

"No," Charlotte said, eyes narrowing. "There's one person none of them will argue with. We're going to Bond Street to see the Gentleman."

Enid goggled, but she hurried to wave over their carriage.

Gentleman Jackson was just locking the door of his salon when Charlotte and Enid arrived. She had never seen the fellow, only heard him described. It was said his physique was so sublime artists and sculptors begged to use him as a model. He was shorter than Matthew and heavier, if the cut of his peacock blue coat was any indication. As he lifted his hat in acknowledgement, she saw that his forehead sloped back toward his dark hair, and his ears stood out on either side of his face.

He replaced his hat and turned. Charlotte moved to block his path.

"Mr. Jackson, please forgive the intrusion. I'd like to

speak to you about a mutual friend."

He glanced from her to Enid and back. "Oh?"

"Yes. Sir Matthew Bateman."

"The Beast of Birmingham," Enid put in helpfully.

Jackson inclined his head. "I know Sir Matthew. I recommended him to your brother, Miss Worthington."

She hadn't been sure he would know her. They had never been formally introduced, after all. But she shared the same auburn hair and grey eyes as her brother. It wouldn't have been difficult to guess her family.

"I remember," she told him. "I'm sure you've heard, then, about this wretched fight between him and Lord Harding."

"I have," he said, tone darkening. "And I like it no better. Sir Matthew has requested my help in preparing, and I will do what I can to see the fight well fought."

Charlotte stiffened. "Then you can't stop it?"

He shook his head. "Not with His Royal Highness sanctioning it. The time and place are already set, a week from today at Wormholt Scrubs by Fulham. Most of the men in London will likely attend. I'm sorry I can't be of more help."

Charlotte nodded and let him go on his way. He had been her last hope. If neither Matthew nor Lord Harding would speak to the prince, she had no faith she could sway His Royal Highness, even if she could find a way to converse with his exalted personage. Matthew was going to have to fight.

But the Gentleman was wrong about one thing. It would not be just the men of London who attended.

"Since when are you and Miss Worthington friends?"

At Gentleman Jackson's question, Matthew nearly dropped his guard. As it was, he had to step back to avoid the boxer's punishing right.

"You know I served as bodyguard to her and her brother," Matthew said, raising his fists and circling. "Likely she feels a certain loyalty."

He'd come to the salon on Bond Street two days after the trip to Gunter's in hopes of practicing. Now he and Jackson were stripped down to shirts and breeches, fists wrapped in mufflers, and feet positioned forward and back. Behind the boxing champion, drawings on the walls laid out proper techniques and impressive stances, while near the door other devotees hurried to divest themselves of their coats and top hats in hopes of following Matthew onto the hardwood floor.

"Loyalty, eh," Jackson mused. He threw a punch. Matthew blocked and counter-punched, but the boxer jumped back in time to escape the blow.

"Loyalty to my sisters, especially," Matthew insisted. "She's helping them enter Society."

Jackson grunted, but from the statement or the punch Matthew landed, Matthew wasn't sure.

He wasn't any more sure of the matter when he put on his coat to leave a while later. For a moment, in the coach yesterday, he'd considered again whether Charlotte might care for him. Why did he torment himself? He'd seen how she interacted with her maid, their family cook Mrs. Hestrine—always polite, always kind and thoughtful. She wasn't so different with him.

Usually.

But once in a while, there was a look in her eyes, a tone in her voice, that could set a man to dreaming.

He snorted, and the couple who had been approaching on Bond Street hastily stepped out of his way. He tipped his hat in apology. The wife smiled. The husband did not.

Well, what did he expect? Even in a fancy new coat and breeches, he would still appear the brute to some. Charlotte had ever treated him as if he might be more. He still didn't understand why she had taken on the role of etiquette teacher to his sisters, but it was clear she cared about their welfare. She wasn't attending his family for his sake.

Was she?

He could call it doubt; he could call it hope. It persisted in raising its head, for all he tried to quell it. He was a baronet now, a knight. That inched him closer to her position in Society. He was doing all he could to be a gentleman. Was it possible Charlotte returned his regard? He had to learn the truth or go mad.

He didn't wait for Charlotte to come up to his study when she arrived the next day. He joined his sisters in the fussy sitting room, where they were making plans for the at home. He tried not to interfere, sitting and watching instead.

Charlotte didn't look his way any more often than was necessary for good company. When she poured tea, she gave him no more than she gave his sisters. She didn't linger in his company before taking her leave, offer him any kind of encouraging look.

He had been right about her feelings for him, or lack thereof, and he had never been less pleased about the fact.

He escorted her to her coach. Gentlemen did that sort of thing, didn't they? She paused, hand on his as he prepared to help her up into her seat.

"You are practicing for the fight, then?" she asked, grey eyes cool.

"Here at the house and with Gentleman Jackson," he answered.

She nodded. "Good. What do you know about your opponent?"

Was she interested? Why did that raise his hopes yet again?

"Only what I've seen and heard," he allowed. "He'll have power behind his blows. Jackson says he tends to lead with his right. The times he's fought at the salon, he's won five times and lost three."

"So, he can be beaten," she said, eyes narrowing as if she was considering strategy.

"Everyone can be beaten," Matthew told her.

Her gaze brushed his. "What's your record?"

"Ten wins, no losses."

Her eyes widened, drawing him in. "That sounds good. Is it good?"

He shrugged, determined not to preen at her obvious admiration. "Good enough. I'm not worried about this fight. You shouldn't be either."

She sighed. "Easier said than done, I fear. But I'm glad to hear you're confident of victory."

He hadn't said that, but he didn't correct her. It was one more fight—one last fight, he reminded himself. Whether he won or lost didn't matter so long as he never had to do it again.

For only when he knew himself to be a gentleman could he begin to think he might earn the love of a woman as fine as Charlotte.

CHAPTER THIRTEEN

After Matthew's reception by the prince and the news of the impending fight, Charlotte wasn't sure what to expect from the at home. She had worked hard with Ivy and Daisy to make it a success. She had sent notes to any lady and gentleman with whom she could claim acquaintance. The sitting room was neat and clean. Ivy had arranged flowers on the mantel and side tables. Tuny had been persuaded to entertain Rufus in the rear yard with one of Ivy's cinnamon buns to console her for missing the fun.

Ivy and Daisy looked lovely in their muslin gowns, Ivy's sprigged in spring green and Daisy's in buttercup yellow. In a duskier green gown herself, Charlotte sat with them as the clock in Matthew's study upstairs struck two, the sound echoing through the silent house.

Daisy's face fell. "No one came."

"Give them time," Charlotte cautioned, though she felt as if she'd eaten a rock instead of eggs and toast that morning. "The members of the *ton* love to be fashionably late."

The knocker sounded for the first time at a quarter past two. The maid ushered the dowager Lady Carrolton and Yvette, Countess of Carrolton, into the room.

"Miss Bateman, Miss Daisy," Yvette greeted them in her musical voice, her figure swathed in a fashionable muslin gown with an excess of flounces. "How grand to see you again. Mother Carrolton, allow me to introduce our hostesses."

For much of the time Charlotte had known Lilith, her mother, Lady Carrolton, had been frail, her face narrow and hollow. Now her eyes were as bright as a crow's. It didn't help that she tended to favor dark colors, though someone, likely Yvette, had persuaded her to don purple-striped muslin today.

"I know Miss Worthington," the elderly woman declared with a voice designed to carry. She leaned heavily on her daughter-in-law's arm as they drew closer. "It's still Miss Worthington, is it not? You're a spinster."

"I am as yet unwed," Charlotte acknowledged, making sure not to sound unsettled by the fact. "But I'm certain I won't be able to say the same for long about the Misses Bateman."

Yvette made the introductions, and the two sat on chairs facing Ivy and Daisy on the sofa.

"Bitter almond," Lady Carrolton announced. "It will do wonders for blotchy skin."

Daisy's hand flew to her creamy cheek.

"I am certain Gregory said bitter almond was a poison, Mother Carrolton," Yvette said with a look of apology to Charlotte and her charges.

Lady Carrolton waved a hand. "Some concessions must be made to attract a husband."

Charlotte was glad when the knocker sounded again.

Indeed, it sounded for more than two hours, as visitors paraded through the sitting room. Some came for gossip, digging for information about the upcoming fight like ravens searching for grubs. Others came from curiosity but stayed to chat. Ivy and Daisy received compliments on their poise, their fashion sense, their lovely home, and their gracious welcome. Ivy was glowing with pride, and Daisy's eyes sparkled.

Charlotte was equally pleased. While none of the high sticklers had deigned to call, enough members of the *Beau Monde* had visited and left clearly impressed. The girls shouldn't lack for invitations in the days to come.

But the visitor who pleased her most was Lord Kendall. The slender marquess arrived near the end of the allotted time, when the sitting room was empty of other guests. Every sable hair of his head, mustache, and beard in place, he bowed over Charlotte, Ivy, and Daisy's hands in turn before flipping back the tails of his navy coat and taking a seat near Charlotte.

"A lovely room," he said.

"Ivy's inspiration," Charlotte replied with a look to her pupil.

Ivy's smile was small and tight as her gaze dropped to her fingers in her lap, fingers pressed so tightly together they might have been a ball of yarn.

"Indeed," he said. "What inspires you, Miss Bateman?"

"Nature," Ivy said, speaking to her fingers. "God made so many beautiful things it is difficult not to be inspired."

"True," he allowed, leaning back in the chair. "Although this room does not remind me of Nature so much as the Greek pantheon. We might as well be sitting on Mount Olympus."

Daisy made a face. "Where's that? The Lakes District?"

Lord Kendall raised a brow.

"We haven't begun studying geography," Charlotte put in smoothly. "But I'm certain Ivy had a particular scheme in mind when she decorated this room." She nudged Ivy's slipper. When Ivy glanced up, Charlotte smiled pointedly.

"Yes, of course," Ivy said dutifully, gathering herself. "I wanted a space that would welcome guests and be comfortable for our family."

"Family is very important," the marquess agreed. "I believe I heard you had a hand in raising your sisters, Miss Bateman."

Now, who had been telling tales? Or had he been trying to learn more about Ivy? Some in the *ton* would have thought Ivy's role with her sisters to be more suited to a nanny. But Lord Kendall's tone seemed admiring.

When Ivy didn't respond immediately, Daisy jumped in. "Ivy was only twelve when our mother died, my lord. I was six. She took care of me and Petunia, who was a baby."

"Commendable," he said, gaze on Ivy. "Do you like children, Miss Bateman?"

Ivy flashed a smile, the warmth of it brightening her countenance, brightening the very room. Lord Kendall blinked in the beauty of it.

"Oh, yes," she said, tone as brilliant as her face. "There's nothing more fulfilling than seeing a little one grow into who she was meant to be."

Daisy smiled fondly at her. "I'm glad you're my sister, Ivy. I don't know what we would have done without you and Matthew."

Lord Kendall's smile faded. "I hesitate to bring up what may be a painful subject, but are you concerned about your brother in this upcoming fight?"

Ivy paled, but Daisy tossed her head. "No. Matthew will win. Matthew always wins."

His mouth quirked. "I'm glad to hear that. I will be sure to cheer for him at the event."

Charlotte eyed him, a daring idea taking shape. "Miss Bateman and I would love to do the same. If only we knew someone who would be willing to take us along."

He straightened. "A fight is no place for a lady, Miss Worthington. If Sir Matthew was here, he'd say the same."

"Sir Matthew is wonderfully broad-minded when it comes to the place of women in Society," Charlotte said brightly. "I realize, of course, that we couldn't go openly. I suppose we could go in my carriage. It is closed. Still, I wonder at the potential danger. Would we be surrounded by ill sorts, do you think?"

"Perhaps not as many as usual, given His Highness's interest in the event," he allowed. "But I wouldn't want you to go unattended."

Charlotte clasped her hands together. "Wonderful! Then we may count on your escort. Isn't that excellent news, Ivy?"

Ivy had been watching the exchange, but with interest or dismay, Charlotte wasn't sure. Now Matthew's oldest sister shook her head at Charlotte before turning to the marquess, who appeared to be trying to formulate a plan of escape, if the furrowing of his manly brow was any indication.

"You do not need to accompany us, Lord Kendall," Ivy told him. "I would not want to inconvenience you or put you in a difficult position."

His brow cleared, and he inclined his head. "On the contrary, Miss Bateman. It would be my honor to be of service. Shall I have my carriage here an hour before the fight? That should give us time to reach Wormholt Scrubs."

"Perfect," Charlotte assured him.

They spoke of commonplaces a moment before he excused himself. Daisy tiptoed to the sitting room door to watch him leave, then turned with wide eyes to her sister. "He likes you!"

Ivy raised her chin. "I'm sure he was only being polite. I know you were trying to help, Miss Worthington, but I cannot like how you manipulated him."

"And gave us an opportunity to see this fight," Charlotte reminded her just as a sound came from the entry.

"Pardon me, madam." Betsy, who had been opening and closing doors all afternoon, sounded testy. "I didn't hear your knock."

"I didn't knock," came a bold female voice. "I don't need to knock at my own door."

Daisy paled and ran back to join Ivy, who had risen. Ivy put her sister protectively behind her. Charlotte rose as well, not sure what she was about to face.

An older woman breezed into the room. Her hair might have been grey, but it certainly hadn't come by the titian color naturally. The red emphasized the black of her plucked brows and the glaring yellow of her rumpled gown, which dipped low enough around the neck so as to leave no question of her figure. She glanced around, reddened lips curling.

"Putting on airs, I see," she sneered. "Well, we'll have no more of that now that I'm here."

"Mrs. Bateman," Ivy said, voice shaking. "This is Matthew's home."

Mrs. Bateman? So, this was Matthew's unlamented stepmother. She sashayed into the room, beaded bag swinging from one meaty fist.

"The Beast of Birmingham," she said in her high, sharp voice. "I remember. But I'm your mother, and I have rights too."

"You're no mother of mine," Daisy declared.

Mrs. Bateman's blue eyes flashed a warning, and Ivy hitched back from her. Enough of that!

Charlotte stepped forward. "Now, Daisy. Remember your manners." She turned to the woman. "Mrs. Bateman. I'm afraid our at home just ended. You'll have to visit another time. If you'll leave your card, we'll let you know when might be convenient."

Matthew's stepmother gaped a moment. "Who are you?"

"This is Miss Worthington," Ivy put in, straightening. "She's sponsoring us for the Season."

Mrs. Bateman's eyes settled on her stepdaughters. "Sponsor, eh? We'll have none of that either. I raised you girls proper."

"Not that sort of sponsor, madam," Charlotte informed her, cheeks heating until they likely matched the red of Mrs. Bateman's hair. "Sir Matthew hired me to help his sisters acclimate to London Society."

"Sir Matthew." The sneer was back on her face and in her voice. "I heard about that. It was in all the papers. His fancy friends won't think so highly of him once I tell them a story or two. Abandoning his poor old mother to fend for herself."

"I'm sure Sir Matthew would be delighted to take up the matter with you," Charlotte said. "At a later time. Betsy! Would you show Mrs. Bateman to the door?"

The maid peered uncertainly through the doorway, but Mrs. Bateman stalked forward and seized Charlotte's arm, fingers digging into her flesh.

"I've had about enough of you, missy. You'll be the one leaving."

Charlotte tried to yank away, but the woman was strong. Though Charlotte dug her heels into the new carpet, Mrs. Bateman managed to tow her toward the door.

"Please!" Ivy cried, running after them. "Don't hurt her. She's been kind to us."

"Because your brother paid her," Mrs. Bateman declared. She shoved Charlotte out into the entry.

Charlotte's slippers skidded across the wood, but she kept her feet and turned. Before she could protest, Mrs. Bateman stabbed a finger into her chest, pushing her back a step.

"Get out, now, before I throw you out."

She was bruised and shaking, but she refused to bow. "Ivy, Daisy, fetch Petunia and Rufus from the yard. Betsy, take Anna and go stay with Mr. Winthrop's staff. We will all leave."

Betsy fled, but Mrs. Bateman's look shot to the girls huddled in the doorway, their faces pinched. "Don't you move, or it will go worse for you. I came for Petunia, and I won't leave without her."

Daisy darted out of the doorway and ran down the corridor toward the rear yard.

"Go," Ivy begged Charlotte. "Daisy will take Tuny and

run. Find them. I'll stay until Matthew gets home."

"Ivy, please come with me," Charlotte pleaded.

Mrs. Bateman raised a fist, to strike Charlotte or Ivy, Charlotte wasn't sure. But the woman addressed herself to Charlotte. "You find those brats and bring them back, you hear?"

"I'll find them," Charlotte said, more for Ivy's benefit than for that of the horror in front of her, "but I will never allow them to enter this house with you in it." She turned and left.

Gentleman Jackson still knew how to throw a punch. Matthew rubbed his jaw as he climbed the steps to his house as evening approached. He braced himself for the excited bay, the click of nails on wood as Rufus ambled to greet him.

But the entry hall was empty and silent.

Tuny was probably playing with the dog in the rear yard, Betsy helping Anna with supper. It wasn't so very late. Perhaps they could all take a walk, and Charlotte could tell him how this at home had gone.

"Matthew," Ivy called from the sitting room. "Could you come in here, please?"

The tremor in his sister's voice raised his hackles. Something was wrong. Head down and hands ready, he barreled into the room.

"'Bout time you got here," Mrs. Bateman said from one of the gilded chairs, and Matthew pulled up short. From the sofa, Ivy sent him an apologetic glance.

"What are you doing here?" Matthew demanded of his stepmother.

"Well, I like that," Mrs. Bateman huffed. "I come all this way to see you, and you can't even ask after my health."

"Because I don't care," Matthew said. "This is my home. You aren't welcome here."

She made a show of leaning back in the chair, bracing her hands over her stomach. "Oh, I don't know. It's not a bad house. I could be comfortable here, especially now that old fuss-pot has left. Miss Worthington." She made Charlotte's last name sound as if it was much longer than it was. "Didn't seem very worthy to me."

Her punch was harder than the Gentleman's. "What happened to Miss Worthington?"

"She left with Daisy, Petunia, and Rufus," Ivy supplied. "I thought I'd better stay until you returned home, Matthew."

Because their stepmother would have taken anything she fancied if left to her own devices.

"Thank you, Ivy," he said. "Go on to your room, if you'd like."

Ivy rose.

"After you've fixed my supper," Mrs. Bateman added. "And unpacked my things. I prefer a room at the back of the house. Less noise from the street."

Matthew's fists clenched. "You can find a bed at the local inn."

She cocked her head. "Shouldn't you be looking for your sisters? Who knows where that so-called sponsor took them? She had a conniving look in her eyes."

He could only be thankful for Charlotte's quick thinking, and her kindness. "Daisy and Petunia will be fine. Allow me to escort you to the door."

"Oh, *allow me*, he says, as if butter wouldn't melt in his mouth." She shook her head, the light catching on the silver she tried so hard to hide.

"Matthew is only being polite, Mrs. Bateman," Ivy said. "I do believe he's right. You'd be more comfortable at an inn."

Mrs. Bateman's lower lip trembled. "You'd throw me out? Your own kin?"

It was on the tip of his tongue to claim her as no kin of his. She'd never shown Ivy or Daisy a drop of kindness, had spoiled Tuny until the girl was old enough to have a mind of her own. What bond did he share with her?

Ivy—generous, sweet Ivy—had other ideas.

"No, of course not," she assured the woman who had tormented her for years. "It's simply that there isn't room."

Their stepmother hitched herself higher. "You and your sisters can bunk up. I'll take whichever room is largest."

"No, you will not," Matthew said. "I'm going for Daisy and Petunia. You will be gone by the time I return, or I'll throw you out myself."

Even if that made him the Beast of Birmingham.

CHAPTER FOURTEEN

"Truly, darling, it's nothing to concern you."

Meredith's hands tightened at her sides. Julian's look was tender, his smile encouraging. He obviously meant to console, but she was already concerned, and waving the matter away did not help.

"You were snubbed," she insisted. "You should have been in attendance at the levee when Sir Matthew was elevated. You have had the prince's ear since the first balloon demonstration."

He leaned back on the sofa beside her, running a hand over Fortune's fur as the cat lounged in his lap. Her eyes regarded Meredith solemnly, as if chiding her for worrying on such a lovely day.

"His Royal Highness is nothing if not mercurial," Julian replied. "Those rising in favor one day fall the next. Look at Harding, reduced to putting on a pugilistic display to regain his place of affection."

"At least you did not have to go so far," Meredith agreed. "But I know your ambitions, Julian. This slight must rankle."

He shifted on the sofa, and Fortune rearranged herself with a disapproving glance. "Not as much as it might have done once. I find myself content."

As if she agreed, Fortune closed her eyes and began to purr.

Normally, Meredith allowed herself to be swayed by her pet's reaction to people and situations. She should be content as well. Yet she could not shake the feeling that something was not as it should be.

The noise downstairs confirmed it.

Fortune's eyes popped open even as Julian frowned and glanced through the doorway. Something thundered up the stairs, as if a horse was galloping toward them. A massive hound plunged into the withdrawing room, dragging Sir Matthew's youngest sister, with Charlotte and the middle sister right behind.

Fortune bolted.

Chaos reigned.

It was some moments before Meredith had everyone sorted. Julian took charge of the invading beast, his hand tight on the leash as he sat on the far side of the room. Petunia stuck to the arm of the chair and spoke encouragingly to her canine protector. The other Bateman girl, Daisy, had seated herself in the opposite corner and seemed determined to glower at everyone and everything. Meredith had never realized how much she resembled her brother.

Fortune perched on the top of one of the glass-fronted cases, tail lashing, and gaze latched on the lumbering beast across the room. Meredith could only be glad the dog's eyesight appeared to be fading. His bulbous nose must have informed him a cat was in the room, but he hadn't done more than tug on his leash since Julian had taken charge of him.

"I'm so sorry, Meredith," Charlotte said again. Her auburn hair had come free from its pins to curl around her face, and her green skirts were dotted with black and tan hair and spots whose origin Meredith did not like contemplating. "Worth closed up the house before he left on his honeymoon and gave most of the staff time off, so I couldn't take the girls there. And none of the hotels we tried would accept Rufus. I didn't know where else to go."

"You are all quite welcome," Meredith assured her, returning her gaze to her pet. "Fortune, however, may not be as agreeable."

"Wouldn't blame her," Daisy said, skirts drawn close. "I wouldn't be agreeable under the circumstances."

"He won't hurt her," Petunia insisted, tugging on one lock of blond hair as she shifted from foot to foot beside Julian. "Rufus is a good dog."

Meredith gave her a smile. "Alas, I fear Fortune requires more than your word on the matter. You have only recently been introduced, after all."

Petunia removed herself from the dog's side to come gaze up at the cat. Fortune's copper-colored eyes focused on her.

"I'm very sorry, Miss Fortune," she said. "Won't you please come down, so we can become better acquainted?"

Fortune continued to eye her a moment, and Meredith held her breath. Ever since the cat had followed her home during one of the darkest periods of her life, Meredith had trusted Fortune's opinion. If the cat was comfortable around a person, that person tended to be worthwhile. If Fortune turned her back, Meredith knew to do the same. Still, the addition of a large, strange hound to the house might have changed everything.

Petunia held up her arms, and Fortune dropped lightly into them.

Meredith breathed.

"There are only two guest chambers at present," she told them as Petunia snuggled the cat and Julian patted the dog. "The Misses Bateman will have to share."

"We usually do," Daisy said with a shrug that reminded Meredith again of the girl's brother.

"But I'm certain Daisy and Petunia appreciate your kindness," Charlotte said with a look to the middle sister.

Daisy sat higher on the chair she'd appropriated. "Of

course. Thank you so much for making us welcome on such short notice, Miss Thorn."

"And for letting us keep Rufus," Petunia added, stroking Fortune's fur.

"Rufus may stay in the house so long as he doesn't trouble Fortune," Meredith warned them. "Otherwise, he will have to make himself comfortable in the rear yard."

"Perhaps we should introduce them," Petunia ventured.

Julian's brows shot up, and he clutched the leash tighter. Charlotte looked to Meredith.

Meredith took Fortune from her young guest. "Miss Petunia, help Mr. Mayes with Rufus. Do not let him loose until Fortune indicates you may."

Petunia hurried around the sofa as if determined to show the cat how companionable an animal the hound could be. Julian, Daisy, and Charlotte looked less enthused. But Julian clung to the dog as he moved forward and Meredith brought Fortune around the sofa.

Rufus's great saggy-skinned head came up, nostrils twitching, and he bellowed a bark. Fortune reared in Meredith's arms, claws digging into the cotton of her gown. Meredith stepped away, ready to release her pet if Fortune sought escape.

"Hush, Rufus," Charlotte scolded.

The dog dropped his head and sighed. Meredith bent and deposited Fortune on the ground a safe distance away. "Fortune, this is Rufus. He will be a guest in our home. Make him welcome."

Daisy shook her head, and Julian quirked a smile, but neither Charlotte nor Petunia seemed to find it odd that Meredith conversed with her pet. She liked them all the better for it.

Fortune stood poised on the floor. Rufus blinked, drooling on the carpet. Meredith hid her shudder. Did he come with his own napkin?

When the dog didn't move, Fortune slipped around one

side of him, keeping her distance as she eyed the massive hound. Other than the twitch of his nose, Rufus gave no sign he'd noticed her.

"Good boy, Rufus," Charlotte encouraged him, and Julian patted the dog's dark back with his free hand.

Rufus' tail gave a thump. As it hit the ground, Fortune pounced on it.

Rufus jerked forward, knocking Charlotte aside, yanking the leash from Julian's grip, and sending Petunia sprawling. Meredith barely swept out of the hound's way as he whipped his body around to see who had attacked him. Fortune dove for cover behind the arm of the sofa.

"Well, that was a surprise," Julian said, retrieving the leash.

"Indeed," Charlotte said, picking herself up and shaking out her skirts.

"It was an ambush," Petunia declared, climbing to her feet. "Rufus never saw her coming."

But he suspected where she'd gone. He paced along the sofa, sniffing and snuffling. As he reached the end, a white-tipped paw shot out and smacked him on the nose. Rufus recoiled, then rubbed the spot against the fabric, leaving a trail of mucus behind.

"The rear yard," Meredith said. "Now."

Petunia hurried to obey, Julian at her side, and Daisy rose to help them.

As they clambered down the stairs, Charlotte opened her mouth.

"If you apologize again," Meredith said, "I will send you out to stay with the hound."

Charlotte snapped her mouth shut. Then she met Meredith's gaze, and they both started laughing. Her friend joined her on the sofa.

Fortune hopped up on the back and slipped down into Meredith's lap as if nothing whatsoever had happened.

"Naughty puss," Meredith said, still chuckling. "What

am I to do with you?"

"I can't blame her," Charlotte said, tucking back her skirts to avoid the smear of damp on the sofa. "I wouldn't like something five times my size invading my home." She shuddered suddenly. "I didn't like Mrs. Bateman invading Sir Matthew's home, and she's only twice my size."

"An inconvenience, to be sure," Meredith said, petting Fortune. "First this fight and now an unseemly relative. At this rate, I cannot see Sir Matthew being embraced by the *ton*."

Charlotte slumped as if suddenly heavy. "And the girls have worked so hard. *He's* worked hard. Yet I feel a reticence in him. This elevation could have been his making, but he does nothing to seize the moment and everything to tarnish it."

Interesting. She'd sensed the same hesitation in Julian.

"Perhaps he doesn't see it as his moment," Meredith said. "Perhaps he was content with who and what he was."

Charlotte sighed. "Then why agree to have me instruct him? I thought he wanted more."

She'd thought the same of Julian. Had she and Charlotte both mistaken their man?

"We want the best for those we care about," she acknowledged. "Is it possible you wanted more for him then he wanted?"

Charlotte drew herself up. "Well, of course I wanted more for him. He's too fine a man to spend his life as a bodyguard. It's not a position of longevity."

Meredith smiled. "I imagine not. And, if I'm not mistaken, that's the sound of Sir Matthew coming to call now. I'll take Fortune upstairs and leave you to make the explanations."

Charlotte shook her head as her friend vacated the withdrawing room. Explanations were certainly in order, yet how was she to explain what had happened at his home? She still didn't know what to make of it. John Curtis had broken her heart with his selfish ambitions, but even he had never been so horrid as Mrs. Bateman. How did one respond to such evil without repaying it with equal venom? She did not want to be that sort of person. And she certainly didn't want Matthew to become that sort of person.

She didn't have time to gather her thoughts much more than that before Mr. Cowls showed him in. Matthew was dressed as he had been when she first knew him—brown coat, brown breeches, shoes scuffed, and neckcloth knotted. It was as if he'd gone back in time, back in character. The only change was his eyes. Where she was used to warmth and concern, now they positively blazed with emotion.

"Are you safe?" he demanded. "Daisy and Petunia? Are they with you?"

"All fine," Charlotte assured him, motioning him to take a seat. "You must have been home." She licked her lips. "Did you…is she…how is Ivy?"

He snorted and refused the chair, pacing about the room instead, each step a thud. "Ivy is a better Christian than I am. I wanted to throw that woman out, but Ivy counseled mercy."

Mercy. She wasn't sure Mrs. Bateman knew the meaning of the word, but she was proud of Ivy for embracing it.

"Perhaps I shouldn't have taken the girls," Charlotte allowed. "But she was so unpleasant."

"That's her nature," he agreed. "She's sweet as sugar to a fellow until he ups and marries her. And then all is bitterness. Da didn't know it, but she'd had two husbands before him. I won't be surprised if she doesn't settle on another."

He forced himself to stop. "Forgive me. You didn't need to hear all that."

"It helps to understand her a little," Charlotte said. "But I still can't abide the idea of her being with the girls."

His smile was grim. "Never fear. I won't let her hurt my sisters again."

Mr. Cowls must have alerted the others, for Daisy and Petunia hurried in then, Rufus conspicuous by his absence. Charlotte could only hope he was safe in the rear yard and not bothering Meredith and Fortune.

"Oh, Matty!" Petunia dashed up and hugged him.

Matthew patted her back, face softening at last. "Easy now, Sweet Pea."

"Did you send her packing?" Daisy asked, hands on hips.

He raised his head to meet his sister's outraged gaze. "Not yet. But she should be gone by the time we return."

Daisy snorted. "Not likely. She'll find a way to bleed us dry."

"Not if I have anything to say about it," Matthew promised.

Petunia pulled back to gaze up at him. "Daisy said she was awful."

Daisy nodded. "You should have seen how she treated Miss Worthington. Grabbed her arm, dragged her across the floor, and tried to force her out the door."

Matthew stilled. It was the oddest thing. She was so used to him standing poised and ready. Now it was as if every muscle in his body had become hard as stone. His look sent a shiver through her.

"She laid hands on you?" he asked Charlotte, voice low.

Charlotte glanced down at the bare skin below her sleeve. Already dark spots were forming, the bruises she'd expected. "She was rather insistent. But I'm fine."

He was staring at her arm. He reached out a hand, then drew back as if afraid the merest touch would hurt her anew. He raised his head.

"Is Miss Thorn amenable to Daisy and Petunia spending the night?" he asked in that same odd voice.

"Yes," Charlotte allowed. "Why? What did you have in

mind?"

"I need to explain the situation to Mrs. Bateman," he said. "I'd rather spare my sisters, and you."

Alarm skittered along her nerves. "Matthew, you wouldn't do anything you'd regret."

He let go of Petunia, who also regarded him with a worried frown, and gathered himself with obvious difficulty.

"No, Charlotte," he said. "I won't do anything *I'll* regret. And I'll do my best not to do anything *you'll* regret. That's all I can promise."

CHAPTER FIFTEEN

S he'd hurt Charlotte.

Matthew focused on taking slow, even breaths as he hailed a hack to return him to Covent Garden. Of all the slights and cruelties his stepmother had inflicted on him and his sisters over the years, he wasn't sure why this one angered him the most. Perhaps it was simply the final indignation.

Perhaps he hadn't come as far as he'd hoped.

The thought chilled him, but even that couldn't quell the fire inside. It had been building for days, since he'd seen Cassidy again, since Harding's insistence on this fight. He only knew one way to let it out. Somehow, he couldn't pity Mrs. Bateman for being on the receiving end.

He found her in the dining room, finishing up part of a roast that had no doubt been meant for the family dinner. She belched as he stopped in the doorway.

"Back so soon? Where is your ungrateful sister? She was supposed to bring back my Petunia."

"I have no ungrateful sisters," he told her, stepping into the room. "I have no patience either. When you've finished eating, you're leaving. And you won't be coming back."

She leaned away from the table and sucked her teeth a moment, watching him. "That so?" she finally said. She thumped on the table and raised her voice. "Ho, girl! Where's that cake you promised?"

He'd have to apologize to Anna for such treatment. Only it wasn't the grey-haired maid who backed through the servant's door swathed in an apron.

It was Ivy.

Matthew strode around the table and took the tray from her hands. His anger must be showing on his face, for his sister recoiled from him, eyes widening.

"It's all right, Ivy," he told her. "I'm not angry at you."

She lay a hand on his arm. "Don't be the Beast."

He wanted to recoil himself at the reminder. "Would you blame me if I was?"

Her smile was sad. She'd blame him. He'd likely blame himself. Yet how else did a man react to such treatment? Wasn't he to protect what was his?

Mrs. Bateman whapped her hand on the table. "If you two are done, I want my cake."

If he hadn't been wearing gloves his knuckles would be showing white. He carried the tray holding the plate with a generous slice of cake—the last of *his* celebration cake—and set it down in front of her. As she reached for the cake, he leaned closer, catching the cloying scent of gardenias.

"You will not see Petunia," he said, voice low and hard. "And you will not mistreat Ivy, Daisy, or any of my staff."

"Your staff?" She laughed as she lifted the plate off the tray. "You wouldn't have this house or staff or a fancy sponsor for your sisters if it wasn't for me."

Matthew shook his head, straightening. "I earned every penny on my own."

She lifted a forkful of cake and raised it to him in toast. "Oh, aye, after I pushed you. You wouldn't have amounted to anything if it wasn't for me. You owe me. That's why you're going to let me see Petunia."

"I owe you nothing."

She swallowed her bite of cake before answering. "As you say. But you'll change your tune soon enough. What would your new friends think if they knew about your father?"

Now, that was a juicy scandal—a knight of the realm whose father had fallen into a ditch drunk and frozen to death by morning. No doubt the prince would regret honoring him. Could His Royal Highness take back the title? Did Matthew care if he did?

She was watching him. He knew the look. Searching for vulnerabilities, weak spots to hit him next. He smiled, and she frowned.

"Do your worst," he said. "I've been down before, and no doubt will be again."

"No doubt," she drawled. "And you're selfish enough to take your sisters down with you."

Fear tried to worm its way into his confidence. He shoved it back. "Whatever happens can be no worse than living with you."

She flamed. "Guttersnipe! You'll never be good for anything."

"Finish your cake," Matthew said. "I plan to escort you to the door." He turned for the corridor.

The glass hit hard, thudding against his shoulder before falling to the floor and shattering. The room was turning as red as it had when he'd learned Charlotte had been hurt trying to protect his sisters, the way the skies had darkened when Cassidy had taunted him in their fight that Matthew came from weak stock. His hands balled into fists. Every fiber of his being demanded that he pay back pain for pain.

"That's right," she jeered. "Do nothing, just like your father. It figures he'd sire a son like you."

His father had started drinking to escape the pain from an injury at the mill. He'd continued drinking to escape the harridan he'd married. Matthew had chosen another outlet—fighting. That didn't make him like his father. He wasn't the Beast of Birmingham. He could have purpose in this world. Charlotte had taught him that.

He was a knight of the realm, a man who, by God's grace,

might someday be worthy of her hand.

"Finish your cake, madam," he said, relaxing his fingers. "It will be the last thing you take from my family."

Matthew came to fetch them home the very next day. Funny how even Charlotte had begun to think of the house off Covent Garden as home. She smiled at the brick façade as she stepped down from the coach.

"And she's really gone?" Daisy asked as they followed Matthew to the door.

"Gone and good riddance," he said, brown coat flexing as he held the door open for them.

Petunia scrunched up her face as she tugged Rufus up the stairs. "How much did you have to pay her?"

Charlotte stopped in the entry hall.

"Better ask how hard did he have to hit her," Daisy said with a laugh.

"That," Charlotte said, "is quite enough."

She wasn't sure who was redder, Matthew or Daisy. His sister tossed her head. "Even a gentleman would protect his family."

"A gentleman doesn't need to resort to fisticuffs," Charlotte maintained.

Matthew eyed her. "That sure of me, are you?"

In truth, she had woken more than once last night, wondering. But seeing him, eyes clear, mouth hinting of a smile, she could not doubt.

"Yes," she said, chin up. "I am."

His smile appeared, bathing her in warmth. "It was a near-run thing, but you're right. In the end, she left with no need for me to raise my voice, or my fists."

Charlotte beamed at him.

He stood for a moment, as if basking in her approval. Then he collected himself and bent to take Rufus from Petunia. "Best you go to your lessons now."

Petunia watched as he ushered the hound up the stairs, then she turned to Daisy. "He likes Miss Worthington."

Charlotte's cheeks were heating, but Daisy shrugged. "I figured that out days ago."

"Your brother and I have the utmost respect for each other," Charlotte said. "Nothing more."

Daisy snorted. "Says you."

She would not continue this line of conversation. "Where is Ivy? We need to discuss strategy."

Somehow, she managed to gather all three girls in the withdrawing room a short time later.

"I expect invitations any day," she told them, moving about the room to straighten a chair, realign a miniature on the mantel. "In the meantime, I'm trying to decide on an appropriate outing that would continue to advance your position among the *ton*. The British Museum, perhaps, if we could be assured of a day when other luminaries were visiting."

"What about something more exciting?" Daisy asked, shifting on one of the gilded chairs. "I heard Vauxhall can be fun, particularly after dark." She looked to her older sister as if for approval.

Ivy frowned, rubbing a hand along the arm of the chair she'd taken. "I'm not sure who told you that, Daisy."

"Sir William," Daisy answered. "When we were standing out at the ball. He made it sound lovely."

The Vauxhall Pleasure Gardens were an interesting diversion. Their beautiful landscapes served as a backdrop to dances, cold collations, and fireworks, but they were also a place for lovers to meet in anonymity after dark. Chaperones had to be careful that their charges were not led astray. She and her charges had worked too hard to jeopardize Ivy and Daisy's reputations now.

"I'll find out the hours for the British Museum," Charlotte said.

Daisy pouted.

Ivy, who had been pale and quiet for most of the discussion, followed Charlotte out into the entry as her sisters headed for their rooms to change. The oldest girl's face was sagging with her shoulders, as though she'd been through a great deal.

"Thank you, Miss Worthington, for protecting my sisters yesterday," she murmured.

"It seems they didn't need much protecting after all," Charlotte demurred. "Everything turned out well."

"Oh, I can assure you your help was very much needed." Ivy shuddered. "Mrs. Bateman can be demanding, and she's not adverse to using force to achieve her ends. Matthew found that out the hard way."

Charlotte stared at her. "Are you saying your stepmother struck your brother?"

Ivy leaned closer and lowered her voice. "I think she threw a glass at him. I found him cleaning it up after she left. But he didn't strike back. He was a gentleman, just like you taught us to expect."

She lay a hand on Ivy's arm. "Oh, Ivy, I'm so glad. What provocation! Yet he held strong. I always knew he had it in him."

Ivy smiled. "Me, too."

Charlotte glanced up the stairs. "He doesn't need more coaching, but perhaps I should speak to him, tell him our plans."

Ivy nodded, and Charlotte picked up her grey skirts to climb the stairs.

He was standing in the study, two chairs pulled up to the fire, as if he had been expecting her. He waited to sit until she took the chair across from him.

"What lessons do you have for me today?" he asked.

"None," Charlotte assured him. "By all accounts, you are in every way a gentleman."

"Perhaps not yet," he allowed, "but I'm trying."

Charlotte cocked her head. "In what way have you

failed?"

"Should I list them all?" He held up his fingers and dropped each in turn. "I'm practicing to fight before half the fellows of the *ton* while the other half wagers against me. I still prefer a neckcloth to a cravat. And I don't have a valet."

"Minor matters," Charlotte said with a wave of her hand.

He dropped his hand. "Even the fight?"

She cocked her head. "If I said no, would you call it off?"

He shook his head, but she thought he looked regretful. "I can't. Word of honor."

"See?" she prompted. "Only a gentleman would worry about his honor."

"Not true," he insisted. "Any real man wants to be known as honorable. Though sometimes I question my honor."

Charlotte frowned. "Why? You are in all ways to be admired."

"You wouldn't say that if you knew what's on my mind right now."

He had to be teasing her. That look was back in his deep, brown eyes.

"You'll only know if you tell me," she replied.

Still he watched her. "I'm wondering what it would be like to kiss you."

My, but it was hot by the fire. Charlotte rose, to go where, she wasn't sure. He stood as well, once more still. Waiting for her to tell him he had fallen in her estimation. The words bubbled up before she could stop them.

"I wonder the same thing about you," she said.

He moved closer, giving her every opportunity to step back, to protest. She did neither. He bent his head and kissed her.

His lips were warm and solid, much like the man. Yet there was a gentleness, a sweetness that filled her, leaving her longing for more. She had to stop herself from wrapping her arms around him and pulling him closer.

He stepped back, watching her once again.

"Well," Charlotte said, "at least neither of us has to wonder anymore."

He smiled, and she only wanted to kiss him again. But that wasn't appropriate. None of this was appropriate. Why couldn't she make herself leave?

"I would say that a lady only entertains a kiss from a gentleman if she has feelings for him," he ventured.

"And a gentleman who kisses a lady ought to have feelings for her," Charlotte countered.

He nodded. "Reasonable assumption."

Her heart started beating faster, as if it would transfer itself from her chest to his pocket, as if it wasn't already there. "What do you suggest, sir?"

He stuck out his lower lip as if considering the matter. "Perhaps we should try that kiss again, just to be certain."

Oh, no. She was already far too certain. She would not, could not, be in love with Sir Matthew Bateman. It broke the rules. It meant giving up parts of her life.

It meant risking her heart again.

Charlotte managed to force her feet to move, backing for the door. "Perhaps we should each consider our motivations, our purpose. I'll return on Thursday. We can discuss the matter then."

When perhaps she had come to her senses.

CHAPTER SIXTEEN

H e'd been struck mad.
It was the only explanation for his behavior that
afternoon. He'd known a few fellows to reel after a blow
to the head. He rather thought this was a blow to the heart.
He'd kissed Charlotte Worthington. And she'd let him.

He wasn't sure why he'd taken the chance. Why she'd
stayed beyond a moment. Leaving him with one question:
what was he to do now?

He pondered the matter as he practiced in the rear yard,
Rufus snuffling about. The bags of dirt Tuny had filled for
him to lift didn't feel nearly as heavy as his thoughts.

Charlotte was right. A gentleman didn't kiss a lady
without expectations being raised. He didn't need a lesson
from her to know that.

"And what have I to offer her, eh?" he demanded of
the hound, dropping the bag onto the rocky soil. "A
knighthood too new to matter and already questioned by
most. A past of violence and regret. A future about to be
marred by the scandal of this fight."

Rufus sat on his haunches, tongue lolling. Matthew
scratched him behind one ear.

He was mad to have kissed her, madder to hope the kiss
had made any difference in how she felt about him. He
was still the man her brother had hired as bodyguard. She
was still the daughter of a viscount. His knighthood had

given him a stature he'd never had before, but it was still a step down for Charlotte to associate with him, much less marry him.

He'd agreed to hire her to help his sisters. That's where he should focus. He'd behave like a true gentleman, ignore this kiss, ignore his feelings. Stiff upper lip and all that.

He truly was mad to think that might work.

By dinner with Meredith and Fortune, Charlotte still had not composed herself. She'd encouraged Matthew to kiss her, had gloried in the feel of his lips against hers. She'd been lecturing his sisters on what it meant to be a lady and thrown all claims to ladyhood to the winds.

And she couldn't regret one moment of it.

"And so the dragon has been vanquished," Meredith said, selecting a Yorkshire pudding from the linen-lined Sevres bowl beside her plate.

"Mrs. Bateman has left," Charlotte agreed, trying to decide on whether to try the roast beef or the potatoes first. "Order has been restored." At least, within the household.

"Then you are making progress with your charges?" her friend asked as a soft body wound its way past Charlotte's ankles.

"Reasonable progress," Charlotte allowed. "Daisy disagrees with me on occasion, but Ivy is all I could ask for in a pupil. She listens to everything I say and puts it into practice, and with such natural grace you would think she'd been to the manor born. If we can overcome her shyness, she will make her mark."

Meredith nodded as if equally impressed. "And Sir Matthew?" she asked, reaching for her goblet.

Is warm, kind, and considerate. Makes me feel clever, beautiful, cherished.

"Appears to have mastered his new role," Charlotte made herself say.

Meredith set down her goblet. "Yet you are unhappy."

Charlotte straightened. "Unhappy? Certainly not. Why would you suggest that?"

Beneath her, Fortune batted at her ankle as if chiding her for the half-truth.

"Because you have pushed those potatoes around on your plate and now flattened them," Meredith said, pausing to take a bite of her own potatoes.

Charlotte stared at the tell-tale smear, then lay her fork down with a sigh. "I'm not unhappy, Meredith. Truly. It's a pleasure to see Sir Matthew and his sisters do well."

"But?" Meredith encouraged.

Charlotte sighed again. "But I begin to question my role in their household."

Fortune pranced out from under the table, head cocked as if considering whether anyone would allow her to jump up near the food and for how long.

Meredith lay down her fork as well and affixed first Fortune and then Charlotte with her lavender gaze.

"Your role is to help Sir Matthew and his sisters accustom themselves to their elevation. If they insist on anything less, I will remove you immediately."

"Not less," Charlotte hurried to assure her. "But perhaps more."

Meredith's eyes narrowed. "How much more?"

Fortune took the chance. She leaped up onto the table and flicked her tail over Charlotte's plate as if blessing it. Meredith picked her up and deposited her on the floor.

Charlotte could prevaricate further. Fortune had made an effective break in the conversation, after all. Yet perhaps it was best simply to have done.

"I allowed Sir Matthew to kiss me," Charlotte confessed. Just saying the words aloud eased the pressure in her chest.

Meredith's generous mouth quirked. "I take it this was not for the purpose of demonstration."

Charlotte laughed. "No. Not in the slightest."

"I see." She picked up her fork and continued eating.

What did she see? What had Charlotte betrayed? She shifted on the chair and felt Fortune shoot past her again.

"It wasn't entirely improper," she told Meredith. "The door was open, the girls just downstairs."

"Of course," Meredith allowed.

"It was only once and not for very long." *Not long enough.*

"Certainly."

"I doubt it will happen again."

Meredith raised a raven brow. "Do you?"

"No." Charlotte blew out a breath. "I fear it could happen again all too easily. I have admired Sir Matthew for some time."

"And you are concerned this admiration might turn into something more," Meredith said, as if stating a great truth.

"Yes," Charlotte admitted.

Fortune hopped back up on the table and eyed Charlotte's plate.

Meredith picked her up and handed her to the waiting footman this time. "Then this position is turning out better than I'd hoped. Carry on, my dear."

Charlotte was still trying to determine how to carry on the next day when Lilith called. This time Meredith and Fortune were both in the withdrawing room when Mr. Cowls showed in Charlotte's friend. Always statuesque, Lilith had emphasized her height today with a blue velvet shako topped with a lustrous ostrich plume. The celestial blue matched the color of her satin spencer and dotted the white muslin of her gown. But her color was as high as her head as she threw a broadsheet onto the sofa between Charlotte and Meredith.

Fortune raised her head off Meredith's thigh to eye it.

"You've assigned her to a monster," Lilith announced.

Charlotte blinked in surprise. Meredith's eyes narrowed

at the Amazon glaring at her.

Fortune pounced on the broadsheet, sending it flying off the sofa. Charlotte bent to retrieve it.

"Good afternoon, Mrs. Villers," Meredith said coolly. "How might I assure you that all is well?"

"You can cancel Miss Worthington's contract immediately," Lilith declared. "I won't have her abused."

Paper in one hand, Charlotte straightened with a frown. "What are you talking about, Lilith?"

Lilith waved a hand. "It's all right there. They were selling the wretched things on the street corners everywhere I went, shouting the news to the skies. Mother read every word twice before taking to her bed. All of London is agog."

Charlotte looked down at the paper. *Prince's Pet Has Teeth*, the headline read, followed by a subhead, *Mother of Beast of Birmingham Tells of Violent Past*.

Cold doused her.

"What does it say?" Meredith asked, voice surprisingly gentle.

Charlotte couldn't make herself read further. She held out the cheap paper, and Meredith took it from her fingers. Her lavender eyes moved back and forth as she scanned down the page. Then she tossed the sheet aside, where Fortune promptly pounced on it again, rumpling it into a ball.

"Rubbish," Meredith pronounced.

Charlotte sagged. "Oh, good. That is, I'm glad there was no truth to it."

Lilith's face was white. "And easy assumption. Villains hide all the time."

Charlotte rounded on her. "Sir Matthew is no villain."

"Are you certain?" Lilith challenged. "His own mother denounces him."

"His mother," Charlotte informed her, "died years ago."

"The Mrs. Bateman quoted must be his stepmother,"

Meredith put in, mouth curled in distaste. "A thoroughly disagreeable person who would like nothing more than to see Sir Matthew suffer. I cannot give her sordid tale any credence."

Lilith's gaze dropped to the carpet, where Fortune was batting about the rumpled paper. "Just because a person is unpleasant doesn't make her a liar."

Lilith had been known for being unpleasant herself, but she was nothing to what Charlotte had experienced with Mrs. Bateman.

"In this case," Charlotte said, "I fear it might."

Lilith took a step back. "I should go. I only intended to warn you. Charlotte, may I have a word with you in private first?"

Meredith rose and gathered Fortune, who had been ripping off pieces of the paper and spitting them out. "I must change for an outing. Take as much time as you like. Mrs. Villers."

"Miss Thorn." Lilith stood, head high, as the employment agency owner sailed past. Fortune stared at her with baleful eyes as if warning her not to try taking back her new toy.

Lilith moved closer to Charlotte, dark eyes troubled. "I know you don't want to believe this story, but I worry for you. This Mrs. Bateman claims Sir Matthew is a brute, beating his sisters and her."

Charlotte felt ill at the very thought. "That cannot be true. His sisters show no fear in his company. On the contrary, they run to him for comfort and advice. They look for excuses to spend time with him, encourage him in every way. Surely that would not be so if he harmed them."

"Perhaps." Lilith twisted the cords of her reticule around her fingers. "But I heard of a man once, a gentleman in every way to his friends and acquaintances, who spoke so harshly and with such cruelty to his wife and daughter that they despaired."

Charlotte shook her head. "That would indeed be horrible, if it was true. You know how the *ton* loves its gossip."

Lilith's shoulders tightened in her celestial blue spencer. "It is no false tale, Charlotte. I experienced it for myself. The man in question was my father."

"Oh, Lilith!" Charlotte pressed her fingers to her lips, not knowing what else to do.

Her friend took a step back as if to prevent Charlotte from offering solace. "It was a nightmare. Mother retreated to her bed and refused to rise. I avoided contact with others, convinced I was the ugly, stupid girl he called me."

Charlotte had to reach out a hand, touch her friend's arm in sympathy. "Did Gregory do nothing?" she asked, thinking of Lilith's gentle giant of a brother.

"Gregory never knew. I thought he must, and I was very angry with him for many years. But I realized later how careful Father was never to show himself in front of Gregory."

"I'm so sorry to hear this, Lilith," Charlotte murmured. "I wish I'd known. I would have assured you that you are beautiful and clever."

Lilith managed a smile. "I had to come to believe it myself. Beau helped. He sees me as a marvelous being, and so I try to be my best self for him."

"I'm glad he brings you joy," Charlotte said.

"More than I thought possible," Lilith assured her. "And I want to see you as happy. Your Beast is not to be trusted. If this woman is telling the truth of what she's seen, you aren't safe with him."

How very strange. From the first time she'd met Matthew, she'd been drawn to him because he made her feel safe. The death of her mother and father had left her shaken, unsure. She and Worth had clung to each other, but she'd soon realized she couldn't fully depend on her brother either. Worth's clever mind led him here and there, like a lark darting on the breeze. She never knew what mad start would move him next.

Matthew was solid, steady, dependable. He had come into her life at a time when she'd been hurt by John Curtis's defection, when Worth had begun receiving notes that threatened death and destruction. Matthew had protected her and her brother, rescued Worth from calamity several times. He'd saved the prince's life!

She could not see him as a bully who terrorized the women in his life. Her heart refused to accept it.

"A villain should not be suffered to succeed," she told her friend. "Bullies must be shouted down. But I am in no danger from Sir Matthew. He would do anything for his sisters. I'd stake my life on it."

Lilith lay a hand over hers. "Be careful, Charlotte, for I fear you've done just that."

CHAPTER SEVENTEEN

By Thursday morning, Matthew was convinced he could behave like a gentleman in Charlotte's company. He would be calm, cool, and sophisticated. That was what everyone expected of a knight of the realm. He should get used to it.

But everything seemed against him.

He still didn't see the need for a valet when he had been dressing himself since he was four. His cravat disagreed that morning. No matter how carefully he handled the material Betsy had ironed and starched, his fingers felt thick. His shirt points wilted under the strain. The thing ended up in a bedraggled knot. When he descended the stairs at last, he was acutely aware of the scuffs on his brown leather boots, the sag in the seat of his brown breeches.

Who was he fooling? For all the prince's ridiculous elevation and Charlotte's hard work and kind instruction, he was still a bruiser, the fellow hauling sacks from the mill, the man grappling in the back alley for gold.

He felt the scowl settling on his face as he ate the porridge Anna served. Ivy and Daisy, sitting down the table from him, exchanged glances as if they noticed it.

He set down his spoon. "I'm no good at this."

Petunia, at the end of the table with Rufus at her feet, frowned at him. "Since when? You can put away porridge with the best of them."

Despite his doubts, he smiled. "That I can, Sweet Pea. But then, you eat your share too."

"And mind that *you* eat it," Ivy put in to their little sister. "Porridge isn't for dogs."

Tuny's hand slipped under the table. "Rufus doesn't mind."

"No, but he won't much like porridge," Matthew told her. "There should be better scraps in the kitchen."

"He eats well enough," Ivy assured them both. She turned to Matthew. "But you're not eating this morning. What's troubling you, Matty?"

He leaned back. "I realize I'm to be an example to you all. I don't feel like I'm doing my part."

That won cries of dismay from his sisters.

"You're a fine brother," Ivy protested, face puckering.

"You treat us better than she ever did," Daisy agreed with a toss of her brown curls.

"We like you," Tuny declared.

Their indignation that he should think otherwise warmed him.

"Not quite a gentleman though, eh?" he said.

"Better than some," Daisy answered. "You wouldn't slight us."

His frown returned. "Who's slighting you?"

"No one of any importance," Ivy said with a look to Daisy. "But I agree with Daisy, Matthew. We've had the opportunity to meet several gentlemen. You outshine them all."

"Except maybe the Marquess of Kendall," Daisy said with a sly smile.

Ivy colored. "Even him. Many gentlemen keep themselves hidden behind a proper smile and polished words. You allow people to see your character, Matty. I find that commendable."

Matthew picked up his spoon, the creamy porridge suddenly looking more palatable. "Too bad others don't think the way you do."

"To quote a gentleman I admire," Ivy said, "what do you care what they think?"

Matthew chuckled. "You three are good to have around. You keep a fellow honest and humble."

Tuny nodded. "That's what we're supposed to do. We're your sisters."

Breakfast tasted finer after that. His spirits recovered, he gave up on perfecting his attire and spent the next hour in the rear yard, practicing.

Many gentlemen on the *ton* practiced their boxing in elegantly appointed salons, where they could boast to their peers about their prowess. Now and then they hired a real pugilist to come spar with them. Lord Worthington had been more practical. He'd converted a room at the top of one side of his double townhouse, roughened the hardwood floors so he wouldn't slip as he moved about, and added cupboards to hold equipment and hooks for hanging mufflers and coats. And he'd sparred with Matthew at least once a day to keep his skills sharp.

Matthew didn't have a spare room or a sparring partner handy. The best he could do was improvise.

He stripped off his coat and hung it on the door handle, then moved out, brittle grass crunching under his feet. Still needed to do something about the yard.

Did knights garden?

He smiled as he took up his stance, feet placed shoulder-width apart, one ahead of the other. Fists raised, thumbs out, elbows close.

Knights didn't garden. They hired someone to garden. Ought to take a gardener an hour to deal with this pitiful patch of grass.

He began punching: right, left, under, over. He imagined a fellow taller and broader than him, considered how to get under his guard, how to stay away from his reach. He danced forward, back, fists flashing.

Humble, remember? Don't be so sure you'll win. Be ready. Be strong.

A movement caught his eye—the door swinging open. Betsy going to the coal shed, perhaps, or Tuny letting Rufus out now that he'd finished his breakfast and hers. He kept punching until his breath came fast and sweat cooled his neck.

But no one passed him for the coal shed, and no hound tried to catch his moving feet. Matthew paused, wiping perspiration from his eyes with one hand, and turned.

Charlotte stood in the doorway, watching. Her grey eyes were wide, her pink lips slightly open, as if her breath came as quickly.

Matthew started toward her. "Is something wrong?"

She snatched his coat off the handle and thrust it at him. "No, yes. That is, we must talk."

Charlotte couldn't catch her breath. She'd seen Worth in his shirtsleeves before, had even interrupted him when he was practicing fencing in his salon at the top of the house. But he was her brother.

And he wasn't anywhere as good at the art of boxing as Matthew.

The grace he displayed as he moved about the yard— the precision, power, and speed of his fists—held her in awe, and she hadn't been able to speak to alert him to her presence.

He took his coat from her and slipped it over his broad shoulders. "Talk? About what?"

Belatedly she realized that she'd promised they would talk about the kiss. That promise had been a mistake. She couldn't talk about kissing him, couldn't stop thinking about kissing him. Didn't want to notice how close he was, how easy it would be to kiss him again.

She made herself open her reticule and draw out the remains of the broadsheet, which she'd rescued from

Fortune and forced herself to read.

"This is making its way around London," she told him, offering him the page. "I thought you should see it before I warn the girls."

He took it and frowned down at the words. His face darkened.

"Lies," he said, shoving it back at Charlotte. "But then, it's part and parcel to who she is."

"I'm beginning to understand that," Charlotte said, accepting the loathsome report. "But the rest of the *ton* may not be so understanding."

"Anyone who believes that rubbish isn't worth my notice," he said.

Charlotte sighed. "Normally, I'd agree, but we must think of Ivy and Daisy. This could affect their already tenuous standing."

"So, what do you want me to do?" he challenged. "If I confront the publisher, I confirm his tale. Isn't a gentleman supposed to be above such things?"

"Yes," Charlotte allowed. "But even a gentleman protests when he's been maligned. Really, the report is scurrilous. She claims your father was a drunk and that you maimed a man."

He looked away. "She's not wrong there."

Once more Charlotte's breath left her. "What?" she managed.

His shoulders tightened, straining the seams of his coat. "My father was injured on the job more than once, but he never stopped working. His way of forgetting the pain was to drink himself into a stupor. I didn't understand when I was a lad, but by the time I was twelve, I thought enough of myself to try to convince him he could do better. The back of his hand was my answer."

Something inside her wept for the boy he had been. "I'm sorry he treated you that way, Matthew."

"I was sorry too, that I'd even bothered to try to help

him. I moved out when I turned fourteen to work at the mill carting goods all over the city. I started fighting when I was sixteen. I lived in the back of the mill, helped at the closest inn for scraps so I could send every penny I earned home to Mum. I didn't want her to worry whether she and the girls would have enough to eat after he'd drunk his pay. Then Tuny came, and Mum left us, and I kept working and fighting to take care of my sisters."

She had never lived such a life, knew no one who had, yet the tale touched something inside her. She reached out, took his hand. "They are fortunate to have you."

"Not so very fortunate," he murmured, but he didn't pull away. "You saw the woman my father married. She gave him more reasons to escape into a bottle. He fell into a ditch on the way home from the public house and froze to death. And the new Mrs. Bateman was only too happy to keep taking my money."

"That's why you brought the girls to London," Charlotte realized.

He nodded. "I agreed to a big fight, a proper fight with a square, bottlemen and kneemen, and umpires. Everyone said I'd lose, and they came to see me beaten. Even my opponent, Mitch Cassidy, the Giant of Lancaster, mocked me. Someone must have told him about my father, because he jeered at me in the square that I was no better. Weak stock, he called us. Drink was the only fuel capable to getting a weakling like me into the square with him."

He pulled away from her. "I'm not proud of what I did that day, Charlotte. It was like my soul cracked open, and a beast emerged. I pummeled Cassidy within an inch of his life, put all my anger into every blow. The umpires had to pull me off him. I won, but he never walked again. He was the acquaintance who died a few weeks ago."

Tears were streaming down her face, for his father, his mother, for him and this Cassidy and the girls. "You were pushed beyond all expectation," she murmured. "Anyone might have reacted the same."

"A gentleman wouldn't," he countered. "A knight of the realm wouldn't. I swore never to fight again, to find ways to atone for what I'd done."

"That's why you took the job protecting me and Worth," she said.

He shrugged, threatening his seams even further. "It was useful, clean work."

"You saved our lives," she told him.

He met her gaze, and his eyes widened. "Charlotte, please don't cry. I'm not that man anymore. I'd never hurt you."

"I know," Charlotte told him. "You're not a beast, Matthew. I'm crying for all the things you and your sisters have had to endure. I'm crying because I don't have the power to go back and make things right, to help you the way you helped me."

He reached out, caught a tear on his finger, his touch as light as a caress. "I want the same thing, to change the past."

Once more she caught his hand and cradled it close. "It's not the past that should concern us. What's done is done. You have another fight coming. You must be ready. I'm going to help you."

CHAPTER EIGHTEEN

She meant it. Matthew had never seen anyone look more determined, more zealous for a cause.

"Thank you," he said, humbled once more. "But I'm not sure what you can do to help."

She was.

"We'll draw up an exercise regimen," she said, sweeping into the house and marching for the stairs, green skirts flapping. "I am familiar with Worth's. And I know you've been practicing with Gentleman Jackson."

"Every other day," he acknowledged as he followed her up to his study.

"Morning or afternoon?" she asked, going to the open secretary and selecting paper and quill.

"Afternoon."

She made a note of that. "We'll need to work on stamina, strength, and speed. Am I missing anything?"

"A willingness to endure pain?" he joked.

She glanced up at him. "If you are that good of a fighter, sir, I expect you to avoid pain."

If only it was that easy.

Nor was it easy to dissuade her, so he gave up trying. He had never known Charlotte to do anything half-heartedly. In that way, she resembled her brother. So he wasn't surprised when she thrust herself into his preparations.

She came over every morning, spending time with his

sisters, then bringing her chronometer out in the yard to time his practices. She was always accompanied by one of his sisters, most often Tuny with Rufus. At first, the dog bayed when Matthew started punching the air, but by the third day the old hound seemed resigned to the fact that this was just another human eccentricity.

Tuny was as serious as Charlotte. The girl had taken to mimicking her mentor, pulling her braids up into a bun and holding her head high. She perched herself sidesaddle on Matthew's back like a princess on her stallion while he raised himself by his arms from the ground.

"Come on, Matty," she encouraged him. "You can push higher."

"You keep growing like a weed, and I won't be able to," he predicted, pressing himself up.

"I believe it is not the height but the repetition that will make the difference," Charlotte said, consulting her chronometer. "That makes twenty-five, twenty-five more to go."

Matthew groaned. Rufus barked in sympathy. At times, he was certain it would have been easier joining a regiment and running off to fight Napoleon.

As if his preparations weren't enough, Charlotte insisted that he accompany Ivy and Daisy to events in the evenings. Since their at home, invitations arrived daily. The dinners weren't bad. The food was good, and the hostesses generally seated him near some Corinthian who was more than happy to discuss boxing or other manly sports. Charlotte was often close enough to give him the eye if he started to forget himself. He hadn't realized it was an insult to her until Daisy brought it up on the way home one night.

"I still don't care for these rules," she announced as the hired coach headed for Clarendon Square to let off Charlotte first. "We were nowhere near anyone else interesting at that table."

"Lady Swelting prefers to seat by precedence," Charlotte

said with a commiserating smile.

Ivy frowned. "Then shouldn't you have been seated higher at the table, Miss Worthington? You're the daughter of a viscount."

Something rumbled through him, like a loaded lorry shaking the ground as it passed. "Was she slighting you?"

Charlotte waved away the thought. "I couldn't care less what people like Lady Swelting think. We had a lovely dinner, surrounded by mostly congenial company. And an invitation from her will raise Ivy and Daisy in the estimation of other hostesses."

Ivy didn't look convinced. Matthew felt the same. He was the upstart. He understood that. Some would never accept him or his family. Charlotte deserved better.

He handed her out of the coach and escorted her to the door of Miss Thorn's house.

"Thank you," he said when she paused on the stoop. "For caring for the girls and putting up with the slurs."

"Patience will win," she promised. "You'll see. Start with running in place tomorrow morning. I want to spend a little time with Daisy first. She seems disheartened."

"Ivy's getting too much attention," Matthew guessed.

"Ivy should get the lion's share," Charlotte said. "She's the eldest."

"I know a lady who should get more," he told her. "You."

In the light of the lamp over the walk behind him, he could see her blush. "That is very kind of you to say, Matthew."

"Kindness has nothing to do with the matter."

She pulled away as far as the narrow stoop allowed. "The girls are waiting. I should let you go."

He sighed and stepped back. "Goodnight, Charlotte. Sleep well."

She hurried inside.

He returned to the coach once more feeling heavy and ungainly. As he settled in his seat, the carriage started for

Covent Garden.

"You should tell her you love her," Daisy said.

"Daisy!" Ivy chided even as Matthew stiffened. "Forgive us, Matty. It's none of our affair."

"It most certainly is," Daisy protested. "Tuny agrees. We both like Charlotte. You ought to marry her."

He glanced at his oldest sister. "You disagree, Ivy?"

She sighed. "I admire Charlotte. Nothing would make me happier than to have her as a permanent part of our family. But I'm not certain she would be as happy. She's a lady, Matthew. She's used to finer things, better reception, than we will ever have."

He couldn't help his flinch. "I know. I think the same."

Daisy glanced between them. "What's wrong with you two? We have a wonderful family. And it's only going to get better from here. Matty's a hero, and everyone will know it after he beats that odious Lord Harding. Besides, Ivy's on her way to marrying a marquess."

"What's this?" Matthew demanded.

Ivy raised her chin. "Nonsense. Lord Kendall is only furthering a friendship."

Daisy started to snort, then turned the sound into a ladylike cough into her gloved hand.

"A gentleman who wants to be friends doesn't look at a lady as if she was better than a cinnamon bun," she informed her sister when recovered. "I saw him at dinner the other night. He might have been way down the table, but his gaze wasn't on the trout."

"Should I be having a word with his lordship?" Matthew asked, glancing from one sister to the other.

"No," Ivy said, and he'd rarely heard her so determined. "I have no way of knowing what's in Lord Kendall's mind, but I can assure you I have no intention of marrying him."

Matthew nodded. "Milksop. I thought so the moment I saw him."

"Matty," Ivy scolded. "Not all men were born to fight."

"You see how she defends him?" Daisy asked. "Admit it, Ivy. You fancy him."

"I will admit no such thing," Ivy declared.

Daisy threw up her hands. "You're mad, the pair of you. I can promise you, when I fall in love, the fellow will have no doubts on the matter, and neither will I."

A wall stood between them. Charlotte felt it every time she was with Matthew. The kiss loomed in the background, begging discussion. Worse, it demanded repetition. She could not bring herself to do either.

She was to be an example to Ivy and Daisy. She knew the expectations of Society, had been raised to meet them. Though she had pressed against the boundaries often enough—by refusing to accept prominent suitors she could not love, by assisting Worth in his studies—she had never knowingly defied them.

Until she met Matthew Bateman.

Her talk with Daisy the next day didn't help. After making sure Petunia was assisting Matthew in practicing in the rear yard and Ivy was working on the embroidery pattern Charlotte had given her, Charlotte took his middle sister aside in the entry.

Daisy shifted on her feet. "Now what have I done wrong?"

"Nothing," Charlotte said, laying a hand on the shoulder of the girl's yellow-sprigged muslin gown. "You seem dispirited of late. How can I help?"

Daisy's frown gathered. "You could stop clamoring on about these rules. Not everyone follows them. *You* don't follow them."

Charlotte drew herself up. "I try. And I would prefer that you see them not as rules but as guidelines that help us behave in a civil manner."

"Is this fight civil?" Daisy demanded, pulling away. "Was

Mrs. Bateman civil? I don't hear her or Lord Harding being read the Riot Act."

"You can be sure Lord Harding has been stricken from a number of guest lists," Charlotte told her.

"And Mrs. Bateman will never be added," Daisy allowed. "Then again, neither will we unless Ivy accepts Lord Kendall."

Charlotte smiled. "Marrying a marquess does generally raise one's status."

"But will that be enough?" Daisy asked. "What, do I have to marry a prince to be accepted?"

"No," Charlotte said. "Nor does Ivy have to marry Lord Kendall. Forgive me if I ever made you think a title meant everything. I have been courted by earls and viscounts, and I refused them all."

"Why?" Daisy asked.

"Because I didn't love them. I would not ask you or Ivy to do less."

Daisy's brow cleared. "Good, for I won't. Just see that you remember the new rule, Charlotte."

"Rule?" It was Charlotte's turn to frown.

Daisy snapped a nod. "A lady marries the man she loves. I expect to hear something about that shortly."

Did she mean about Ivy? She must mean Ivy. Charlotte wasn't ready for anything else.

She was never more aware of her conflicted feelings than on the day of the fight. She was on hand to encourage Matthew before he headed to the big event, standing in the sitting room with Ivy, Daisy, Petunia, and Rufus. Each of his sisters gave him a kiss. Rufus licked his hand.

As Matthew paused before her, she knew what she should do—extend her hand, offer her best wishes, smile politely.

Instead, she reached up and adjusted his neckcloth. It was

one like many of the pugilists wore, a brilliant blue with spots of color that reminded Charlotte of the feathers of a peacock.

"Be careful, Matthew," she murmured. "Come home safely to us."

As she lowered her hand, he caught it in his. "Always," he said, voice solemn. He brought her hand to his lips and kissed the back.

A tremor shot through her.

He let go, stepped back, gave them all a confident smile, and strode out the door, taking Charlotte's heart with him.

Petunia ran to the window. "There's the coach. It's got a fancy picture on the door—lions and a unicorn."

Charlotte blinked, then joined Ivy and Daisy in hurrying to the window.

"That's one of the royal coaches," she told the girls.

"Maybe the prince is inside!" Daisy cried.

They didn't have a chance to find out, for the liveried groom opened the door for Matthew, closed it behind him, and climbed back onto his perch before the coach set off.

Daisy sighed.

Charlotte stepped back. "Hurry, now. Lord Kendall will be here any moment. Ivy, fetch your shawl. Daisy, I trust you to look after Petunia and Rufus and the house."

As Ivy hurried out, Daisy nodded, though her lips curled down. "I wish I could come too."

"There's hardly room in one of those coaches," Petunia pointed out. "Besides, you want his lordship to be looking at Ivy and not you, right?"

Daisy nodded again. Charlotte was just glad Ivy had left the room and had been spared the conversation.

In all truth, she wasn't entirely sure why the marquess was going to such trouble for them, her manipulations notwithstanding. He and Charlotte hadn't moved in the same circles when she had had her Seasons, but she and Meredith had consulted Mr. Cowls about the fellow, so she knew more than she probably should. His was an old and notably fussy family, though both parents were now gone. He had married almost two years ago in what many had considered a love match, only to lose his wife in childbirth ten months later. His daughter could be no more than seven months now. If he had loved his first wife as much as had been rumored, it seemed unlikely he would be seeking a bride again so soon. Yet why else befriend Ivy?

She and Charlotte were ready when his coach drew up a short time later. He came to the door himself, dressed in the requisite navy coat and fawn trousers of a gentleman of the *ton*. Once again, Charlotte tried to imagine this bastion of tradition with the Bateman family.

That he was uncomfortable was evident by the way his brown eyes dipped down at the corners. Still, he bowed over their hands politely enough.

"Are you certain I cannot dissuade you, Miss Bateman?" he asked, straightening. "Though this is an exhibition match before the prince, I expect it could become distasteful to a young lady like yourself."

Ivy glanced at Charlotte, then straightened her spine in her green sprigged muslin gown. "It may well be distasteful to me, my lord, but I want to support my brother in all he does."

"Shall we?" Charlotte urged.

Smile overly polite, he escorted them out the door.

Wormholt Scrubs proved to be a grassy area some distance to the northwest of Mayfair. Much of the commons had been enclosed, but enough remained to allow a good-sized crowd to gather. Fine carriages circled the space, with rougher wagons drawn up beyond. Lord Kendall's driver managed to find a spot opposite the carpeted dais that had been erected for His Royal Highness, who sat on a crimson-upholstered, high-backed chair surrounded by his set and the yeoman guards.

Between the prince and the coach lay a roped off area

approximately ten feet square. The grass inside had been tamped down, as if crushed by the movement of many feet. At one of the corners nearest the prince, Matthew stood with two other men. He had divested himself of coat and neckcloth, his linen shirt open partway down his chest. Charlotte wasn't sure which was more shocking, his dishabille or his companions. One was the Earl of Carrolton, his size making even Matthew look slight. Charlotte stared at the other.

"I didn't realize your brother had aligned himself with Sir Matthew, Miss Worthington," Lord Kendall said.

"I didn't realize Worth was back from his honeymoon," Charlotte replied. Why hadn't he let her know? Why hadn't Matthew let her know? Or had her brother simply breezed into town in his usual burst of energy and appeared at Matthew's side today?

She glanced around and spotted her brother's coach at the back of the grounds. Surely her sister-in-law Lydia wasn't inside. Even the bubbly blonde might be daunted by this exhibition.

For it was clear that not only the wealthy and privileged had patronized the fight. Men in rough coats bumped elbows with lords in tailored jackets. Voices rose and fell in a buzz like a hive of bees. Over the noise came the call of vendors hawking roast nuts, oranges.

And offering odds at five to one in Lord Harding's favor. Charlotte tried not to bristle at that.

The lord in question was making his way to his own corner, opposite Matthew's. He too brought two gentlemen with him. Voices called, encouraging him. From before the prince, two more men entered the square, their size and stride marking them as pugilists as well. Once more Charlotte could only stare as both Matthew and Lord Harding pulled their shirts off over their heads, leaving their chests bare. Her mother would have fainted to find her here.

She was dimly aware that conversation continued inside the coach.

"Has your brother explained the process, Miss Bateman?" Lord Kendall asked.

Ivy, closest to the window, shook her head, gaze on the crowd outside. "No, my lord. I would appreciate any insights."

He shifted on the seat, cutting off Charlotte's view. "Each opponent has two helpers, as you can see."

Charlotte leaned around him. Lord Carrolton had gone down on one knee, and Matthew took a seat on the other, while one of Lord Harding's helpers did the same for him.

"One is the kneeman," Lord Kendall went on. "He serves as a stool of sorts between rounds."

How extraordinary. "Why not simply bring a chair?" Charlotte asked.

He glanced back at her. "Because, Miss Worthington, there must be nothing else in the square the fighter might use to his advantage."

Had one fighter once taken a chair to the other? How horrid. She could not imagine Matthew being so brutal.

"And the other helper?" Ivy asked, voice still pleasant, as if she asked about some theoretical subject.

"The bottleman," Lord Harding explained. "He provides water or other refreshment as needed. He may administer aid as well."

Charlotte tried not to think about Matthew needing aid. He'd always won before. Surely, he'd win again today.

One of the two pugilists moved to stand before the prince. "Everything ready, Your Highness. Can we start?"

Prinny waved a chubby hand. "Proceed. And may the best man win."

The umpire stepped back. "Lord Harding, Sir Matthew, take your places."

Each rose and moved to the center of the square. Bare skin gleamed in the summer sun. A hush came over the crowd. Charlotte felt it too. The waiting, the expectation, the knowledge that something powerful was about to happen.

Matthew lifted his bare-knuckled fists, stood one foot ahead of the other. She'd seen him take up the stance any number of times in practice. This time was real. This time he could be hurt. Her heart thumped against her ribs.

"Begin!" the umpire shouted before jogging back out of reach.

Lord Harding circled right. Matthew kept his fists at the ready. Harding swung. Gentlemen cheered. Matthew blocked easily. The common folk shouted their approval. Charlotte took a deep breath.

The opponents edged around each other. Again Harding swung, and Matthew blocked, to accompanying shouts from the crowd.

"It's like a dance," Ivy marveled.

"A deadly dance," Lord Kendall said. "Harding is testing your brother, Miss Bateman, looking for any weakness."

Charlotte raised her head. "He won't find one."

Lord Kendall glanced back with a smile. "Your faith is commendable, Miss Worthington."

All at once, Harding rushed at Matthew, fists pounding at ribs, stomach. Charlotte pressed forward, willing Matthew to push him back. Matthew gave way, blocking, blocking, protecting. Then one fist shot out, catching Harding on the jaw. Down went the proud lord. She was certain the carriage shook with the impact. No more so than she was shaking.

"Halt!" shouted one of the umpires, shoving between the two fighters.

Matthew stalked to his corner, but he didn't sit on Lord

Carrolton's knee. His face was hard, set. The ferocity of it pushed her back from the window, even as the crowd took up the chant.

Beast! Beast! Beast!

Who was this man?

CHAPTER NINETEEN

Meredith shuddered as Lord Harding rained blows on Sir Matthew, but she couldn't help her nod of satisfaction as the knight's fist connected with the fellow's jaw.

"Bloodthirsty, aren't you?" Julian drawled.

She smiled at him over her shoulder. Julian was seated behind her on the bench of his coach, watching around her, a steadying presence. It had been gratifyingly easy to convince him to take her to the fight. She only wished she'd felt comfortable bringing Fortune, but she couldn't risk losing her pet in the crowd should the door open.

"I'm not in the least bloodthirsty," she assured him. "I prefer to think of it as championing justice. Lord Harding is a bully."

"He likes getting his own way," Julian acknowledged. "But I doubt this was what he had in mind when he challenged Sir Matthew."

Indeed not. Harding had risen and was sitting on the offered knee of his kneeman, while his bottleman attempted to check what had to be a painful jaw. Harding pushed him away, eyes narrowing on Sir Matthew, who hadn't deigned to sit.

"Time," called the umpire.

Lord Harding rose and joined Sir Matthew in the center of the square. The call to begin hadn't even echoed before the lord threw himself at the former pugilist.

Meredith had to look away from the flying fists, but she couldn't close her ears to the grunts of pain or the cries of the crowd at every interchange.

"Stupid," Julian said. "Harding's leaving himself open. It's well known Sir Matthew can grapple with the best. His lordship would be wiser to stay back."

There was a thud, and the crowd cheered. She could scarcely hear the cry of "Halt!" over the noise.

Julian touched her cheek. "Would you like to leave?" he asked, concern in his voice.

Meredith made herself look at the square. Lord Harding was climbing to his feet, shaking his head as if to stop it from ringing. Sir Matthew stood beside Lord Carrolton, sipping from a silver cup Lord Worthington had provided. Doubtless it held water, for she could see the clear glass decanter off to one side, sparkling in the sunlight.

"No," she told her beau. "If I'm to see to Charlotte's best interests, I have to know how Sir Matthew takes this fight."

"Whether he wins or loses will be in all the papers," Julian pointed out.

"It doesn't matter whether he wins or loses," Meredith replied. "It matters how he fights."

"Time!"

The two men returned to the center of the square. Now Lord Harding sported a swelling eye. At least it matched his swelled head. He seemed to have learned his lesson about engaging, however, for he stayed out of Sir Matthew's reach. Meredith could see his lips moving.

"He ought to save his breath," she said.

"He's likely hurling insults at Sir Matthew," Julian said. "It's an old trick. The angrier you are, the less likely you are to think clearly."

"Cheater," Meredith said.

But though Sir Matthew's face turned florid, his composure did not crack. Indeed, the only time his gaze left his opponent was an occasional swift glance toward the foot of the field.

Meredith shifted, trying to see what drew his attention. The crowd was no thicker, no more enthusiastic. Indeed, she wasn't sure it was possible to be more enthusiastic. Lords and paupers were cheering him now. Those who had supported Lord Harding were slumping, faces dark. Surely, he wasn't looking at them. The coaches just beyond, then? She recognized the various carriages of the wealthy houses, including that of the Marquess of Kendall.

Lord Kendall. With Ivy perhaps? And Charlotte.

Her client hadn't mentioned she would be attending, but of course, she would do what needed to be done. Meredith's satisfied smile was interrupted by a groan from the crowd, followed by hisses and boos as the umpire cried "Halt!"

"What happened?" she demanded, trying to see through the milling men.

"Harding was lucky," Julian said, voice grim. "He landed a punch to Sir Matthew's ribs. I wouldn't be surprised if one broke."

Meredith winced.

Sir Matthew gave no indication he was hurt, again refusing the knee but accepting the cup Lord Worthington offered. As soon as the umpire called to begin, he strode to the middle, face set and terrifying to behold.

The crowd quieted enough that she could hear Lord Harding's taunt.

"Water doesn't satisfy, does it? You need a drink. Just like your father."

The crowd's disapproval was palpable. So was Julian's.

"Knock. Him. Down," he urged.

Instead, Sir Matthew lowered his guard.

The crowd gasped, shouted for him not to give up. Clearly confused, Lord Harding hesitated.

Sir Matthew smiled at him. Took a step closer.

Lord Harding took a step back.

Now the crowd laughed, jeering at the haughty lord.

Harding lowered his head and charged.

Sir Matthew twisted to one side and slammed his fist into Harding's jaw. Lord Harding plowed the field.

Meredith closed her eyes. She wasn't sure she took a breath before the umpire sent Sir Matthew to his corner.

"This is horrid," she declared, turning to face Julian. Her beau's face was flushed, his eyes bright, as if he was enjoying every minute.

"This is bare knuckles brawling," he countered. "And rather tamer than some matches. Hair pulling and eye gouging are allowed, you know."

Meredith felt ill. "I had no idea. Why would anyone willingly watch, much less take part?"

"The best matches pit skill against skill," Julian explained. "Two warriors battling to the end."

"Lord Harding has no interest in battling," Meredith said. "He wants to humble Sir Matthew, drive him into the ground."

"No doubt Harding thought this a good way to put Sir Matthew in his place," Julian allowed. "It's not easy keeping His Highness' attention."

Meredith could not bring herself to watch as the two men regrouped, focusing on her beau instead. "Still, I begin to wonder about Sir Matthew. Charlotte was certain he was a gentleman, that that scurrilous story in the broadsheets was false. Can a man be so violent in the boxing square but a gentleman at home?"

"Can a man be cunning in business or law, and yet, unaffected at home?" Julian asked. "I pray the answer is yes, for that is my life."

His face had bunched, his tone turned rueful. He worked hard for his many prestigious clients, but she was sure there were times they asked him to do things that challenged his honor.

Meredith touched his cheek. "In any endeavor, there is a line that cannot be crossed, or we risk our character. I have never known you to cross it. You are by all accounts respected by your friends."

His tension eased. "As is Sir Matthew. Why else would Worth and Carrolton align themselves with him?"

There was that. She knew both lords to be good men. Fortune had approved of them. Fortune had approved of Sir Matthew long before his elevation. She had never known her pet to be misled.

"Then, no matter the outcome, you believe our newest knight to be a gentleman of honor?" she asked.

Julian took her hand and held it close. "I do. And I hope you believe the same of me, Meredith."

The look, so tender, so hopeful, was her undoing.

"I do, Julian," she murmured. "Like Sir Matthew, we may struggle to find a place in Society, but we will remain true to ourselves and our love." And she sealed the statement with a kiss.

His rib was on fire, his arms ached, and one eye was beginning to swell, but Matthew didn't care. Harding had done all he could to anger him, striking ruthlessly, jibing about his family, his father. Matthew remained clear-headed. He had left the Beast of Birmingham behind.

If only he could be sure Charlotte wasn't watching.

He'd spotted the Marquess of Kendall's coach as it pulled up, but the flash of a pale face in a bonnet in the window had shaken him more than Harding's blows. Kendall had brought a lady with him. Ivy? Charlotte? Or both?

The idea kept intruding as he blocked Harding's progressively weaker onslaughts. This had been by far one of his less brutal fights, but neither Ivy nor Charlotte would realize that. Knowing Ivy, she would find a way to match the fighter with her beloved brother. But Charlotte?

Seeing him like this would only raise her doubts about him. If he wanted a life with her, he had to end this.

He waited, watching, until Harding's arm wound up and careened toward him. Matthew dodged, the wind of the punch fanning his sweating face. As his lordship's arm swung back, Matthew came up under it and connected with his chin. The blow reverberated up Matthew's arm.

But Harding went down, and he didn't rise.

The umpire bent beside him, checked his neck.

For a moment, panic threatened. But he couldn't have permanently injured the fellow. Not this time. This time, he'd fought like a gentleman.

The umpire stood. "He's out. I declare Sir Matthew the winner!"

The crowd cheered. Lord Harding's bottleman and kneeman rushed forward to see to him.

"He'll demand a rematch," one warned.

Time to end that as well. He knew what Charlotte would want him to do. He held up his hands, turned from side to side. Slowly, the crowd quieted.

Matthew faced the dais. His Royal Highness was all smiles, face as flushed as if he'd been in the square himself. He put his thick hands together and applauded Matthew, and the men around him joined in.

Matthew swept him a bow, though his rib protested. "Your Royal Highness, thank you for your gracious attendance. I have been proud and honored to be your champion."

As Matthew straightened, the prince inclined his head. "My most excellent champion."

"And, in your honor," Matthew continued, voice echoing, "I retire from the field forever. Undefeated, undaunted, like our prince."

The crowd roared its approval. Among the hubbub rose calls of "God save the prince!" "God save England!"

The prince beamed his pleasure.

Matthew would have decamped right then, but the men surged forward, vaulting the ropes to wring his hand, pat his back, declare him a jolly good fellow. He lost sight of Lord Worthington, though Lord Carrolton's grin was evident over the heads of most there. Matthew had been through all the accolades before, but this was sweeter, cleaner.

This was the end, and the beginning.

Beyond the crowd, Lord Kendall's carriage rolled around the square to leave the area. As it passed, Matthew once more caught a glimpse of a face at the window.

Charlotte's face.

She had seen the last of the Beast of Birmingham. Would she see the gentleman he had become?

CHAPTER TWENTY

What a horrid, horrid sport. As Lord Kendall's carriage headed back into London, Charlotte could not erase the image of Lord Harding falling under Matthew's fist. It was as if she'd felt the blow herself, and all of her hurt.

"Your brother is to be congratulated on his victory," Lord Kendall was telling Ivy. "Seldom have I seen a more magnificent display of the manly arts."

Charlotte's stomach roiled, but she was not so far gone as to miss the pallor on Ivy's face.

"I found it difficult to watch," Matthew's sister said, fingers wrapped around each other in her lap.

"It is difficult to reconcile the Beast of Birmingham with Sir Matthew Bateman," Charlotte agreed.

Ivy glanced up to frown at her. "Why? It's just a name. It isn't Matthew."

She wanted to believe that. Every reminder of his past added another brick to the wall between them. His life was so different from hers. He came from a home marred by excessive drink and violence. The father who should have protected him had curled in on himself. The stepmother who should have comforted him had offered only criticism and burden. How did light shine in such darkness?

Lord Kendall had no trouble seeing the fight as something valiant.

"Your brother behaved in every way the gentleman,"

he was assuring Ivy. "Indeed, it was Lord Harding who appeared the beast."

Charlotte couldn't argue that. Too often, Harding's face had been contorted by anger and hatred. Had he no better way to settle differences than to cause someone else pain?

Lord Kendall continued to enthuse, Ivy to nod and smile. Charlotte sat, feeling alone and wanting only to talk to Matthew, to assure herself he was still the man in whom she had believed.

It was forever and a moment before the coach drew up before the Bateman home. Lord Kendall climbed down onto the pavement to hand Charlotte and Ivy out.

"Thank you so much for your escort, my lord," Ivy said.

The marquess smiled. "It was my pleasure, Miss Bateman. Perhaps I may call tomorrow to offer my congratulations to your brother?"

Ivy nodded, but her smile said she knew his congratulations were only an excuse to call. "I'm sure Matthew would appreciate that."

The door of the house banged open, and Daisy flew down the steps, yellow-sprigged skirts flapping. "Don't send him away! We need the carriage!"

Charlotte stiffened, but Ivy stepped between her and Daisy. "What's happened?"

Daisy's brown eyes were wild, her hair falling from its bun on the top of her head. "It's Petunia. She left hours ago to take Rufus for a walk, and she never came back."

Ivy sucked in a breath, then turned to Lord Harding. "Please, my lord, will you help us?"

"Whatever you need," he promised, face once more in its usual solemn cast. "I am at your disposal."

Charlotte caught Ivy's arm. "We mustn't panic. She's a clever girl."

She was surprised to see the set to Ivy's face. Where she had expected to find fear, she saw only determination.

"I know," Ivy said. "And Rufus is with her."

Daisy snorted. "Fat lot of good he is."

"More than you might think," Charlotte told her. "Have you checked with Mr. Winthrop, the neighbor who gave Rufus to her?"

"No," Daisy admitted, shifting her feet beneath her muslin skirts. "I'll send Betsy."

"We'll drive around the area," Charlotte said. "Daisy, stay at the house in case she returns while we're out."

Daisy nodded and went back inside. Lord Kendall handed them into the coach and asked his driver to amble through the various lanes around Covent Garden.

But though they crisscrossed the quarter several times, they caught no sign of a ten-year-old with sunny blond hair and an aged hound at her side.

"Does she have a friend to whom she might go?" Lord Kendall asked. "A relative nearby?"

Ivy's gaze met Charlotte's, and Charlotte knew what she was thinking.

"There may be one person," Charlotte allowed, "but I doubt Petunia would go to her willingly. Do you know where Mrs. Bateman is staying while she's in London, Ivy?"

"Yes." Ivy's voice was small and tight. "But I would rather not introduce her to Lord Kendall."

"Mrs. Bateman?" he asked, glancing from one to the other.

"Sir Matthew's stepmother," Charlotte explained. "A thoroughly unpleasant person who in no way reflects on the kindness, generosity, and amicability of her stepdaughters. And I agree, Ivy. We should not approach her without your brother at our sides."

Ivy sagged. "Thank you, Miss Worthington."

Charlotte turned to Lord Kendall, who was watching with a slight frown on his handsome face. "Which begs the question, my lord. Do you know where the prince expected Sir Matthew to celebrate his victory?"

His frown only deepened. "Most likely Carlton House,

the prince's residence in London. But I was not privy to the plans. As a member of the opposition party, I am not generally welcome at Carlton House."

"I doubt I will be either," Charlotte said.

He stiffened. "Most assuredly not." When Ivy's brows rose, he hurried on. "That is to say, Miss Worthington, no ladies will be present at the victory celebration. Of that I am certain. I cannot in good conscience recommend you attend."

"And I cannot in good conscience do otherwise," Charlotte told him. "Sir Matthew must be informed."

Lord Kendall tugged at his cravat. "Perhaps a servant, then."

"Who will be ignored," Charlotte insisted. "You know these gentlemen, my lord. We are the only ones they cannot dismiss."

He made a face. "His Highness will not be pleased."

"I couldn't care less what His Highness feels right now," Charlotte said. "Have your coachman take us to Carlton House straight away. We must see Sir Matthew, even if that means bearding the lion of England in his den."

Matthew smiled and nodded at yet another toast to his victory. The prince had insisted on feting him and thirty or forty of His Highness's closest friends at the opulent palace that was Carlton House. Lord Harding had not been invited. In the past, a few of the other pugilists had entered the ornate halls when serving as bodyguards for various dignitaries. They'd told tales of marble and gilt, Chinese and Egyptian décor, but those tales could not do the place justice.

The great eating room, they called this. He wasn't sure what anyone was expected to eat. So far only drink had been flowing. There was no dining table in sight, but this room had more crimson draperies than Matthew had ever seen. The great swags, fringed in gold at least a foot long, encircled the room and ran three deep over the windows. The walls, where they could be seen around the huge paintings, were covered in the same crimson-patterned fabric. Each chair lined up down the middle of the room and the sofas along each wall were upholstered in crimson, with fanciful gold arms, backs, and feet. About the only things that weren't gold or crimson were the thick, light blue carpet at his feet and the massive crystal chandelier that fell from the center medallion of the ceiling. Which was also plastered in gold.

Great waste of money, they ought to call it.

None of the other gentlemen seemed to mind. Conversation was growing louder, laughter more frequent, faces more florid. He'd requested water and sipped sparingly. In truth, when he finished a fight he often felt as if he'd fallen into a hole, weariness and aches wrapping around him. Today it was more than that. He could not forget the anguish on Charlotte's face as she'd left the match. He might have beaten Harding, but he might have lost her.

A servant hurried up and spoke to one of the lords closer to His Highness. The dark-haired fellow turned to the prince.

"Your Highness, Lord Kendall is without and requesting a word with Sir Matthew."

The prince chortled. "Even the opposition seeks to congratulate my champion. Allow him to enter."

Two more footmen—liveried in crimson, of course—strode to open the double doors on one side of the chamber. Most gazes swung that way. Standing in the entrance was Lord Kendall, head high, mustache neat, face its usual solemn mask.

Charlotte was at his side.

"Who's that?" the prince demanded, squinting.

"I believe that's Lord Worthington's sister," one of his cronies supplied.

"Can't be," the prince maintained. "She's a clever thing. You won't find her with this lot."

Matthew was on his feet, but careful to keep from turning his back on the prince. "My lord, Miss Worthington."

Charlotte moved down the room so quickly the marquess had to scramble to keep up. Her gaze, however, was on the prince. She stopped beside Matthew and dipped a curtsey.

"Your Highness, please forgive this intrusion. Sir Matthew is urgently needed."

Foreboding dropped like a stone into his gut. He had to clamp his lips together to keep from demanding to know what had happened.

The prince waved a hand. "He is urgently needed here as well. Haven't you heard? My champion was victorious."

That raised another round of "here, here," and "jolly good fellow" with goblets raised and drained.

"Anyone with any sense would have expected as much," Charlotte allowed when the noise finally quieted again. "And because he is your champion, I know you will allow him to rise to the occasion now and be the hero his family needs."

His family? Despite his reservations, Matthew took a step. Charlotte shook her head once. Warning him. Was he always to skate on such thin ice in Society?

"Hero, eh?" the prince mused.

"Certainly a hero," Charlotte maintained. "The man who saved our gracious prince's life, who triumphed over his enemies, who added a note to the legacy that is our noble prince's birthright."

"Doing it too brown," Matthew said out of the corner of his mouth.

The prince didn't look any more impressed.

Lord Kendall glanced between Matthew and Charlotte, then faced the prince. "Forgive me, Your Highness. I cautioned Miss Worthington that this approach would do no good. You are known as the Prince of Pleasure, after all.

We'll leave you to your little party."

"Little party? Little party!" The prince rose from his seat, and all voices went silent. Every gaze latched onto Lord Kendall, some rueful, some sad, most gleeful. Boxing wasn't the only blood sport in the prince's court, it seemed.

"I will have you know, sirrah," His Highness thundered, "that my champion is everything Miss Worthington made him out to be—a hero, a knight of the realm. His valor, honor, and loyalty are unassailable. I can only question yours."

Lord Kendall bowed. "Forgive me, Your Highness."

The prince flipped up his velvet coattails and plopped back into his chair. "Out, Kendall. I do not want to see your face. Miss Worthington, you may borrow Sir Matthew, but I expect a good report of his next heroic deed."

Matthew bowed. "Once more you honor me, Your Highness."

The three of them backed from the room.

"Thank you," Charlotte said to Lord Kendall as the doors closed on voices rising yet again. "You risked much for us."

"Anything for Miss Bateman and her family," Lord Kendall assured her. Indeed, for the first time, Matthew caught a hint of a smile from the fellow, as if his performance pleased him.

Matthew turned to Charlotte. "What's this all about? Were you just trying to rescue me from that, or is something truly wrong?"

Charlotte lay a hand on his arm, the touch both buoying and sinking his spirits. "Very wrong. Tuny is missing, and we fear Mrs. Bateman is to blame."

This room held less crimson, the draperies only falling from the tall windows on their left, but he felt as if they squeezed the very air from the long antechamber. "She's still in London?"

"Ivy knows her location," Charlotte promised. "This way."

In short order, they were seated in the marquess's carriage and headed toward the outskirts of London, while Charlotte explained the situation.

"You were right to fetch me," Matthew told her when she finished. "Mrs. Bateman raised Petunia from a babe. She considers her a daughter. And she knows I'd pay for her return."

Lord Kendall shifted on the padded leather seat. "Surely you don't imply kidnapping."

"Surely he does," Charlotte told him.

Ivy hunched in on herself. Why? His sister was everything kind and good, but surely even she couldn't justify the behavior of the woman who had made her life so difficult. Then again, perhaps her gentle heart couldn't admit the truth about their wicked stepmother.

Matthew was glad when the carriage rolled into the coaching yard of an inn and stopped.

"Stay here," he said, throwing open the door. "I'll be back."

"You're not going without me," Charlotte said, gathering her skirts to follow.

Matthew blocked her exit. "You may not like what you hear."

Her face was pale, but her grey eyes were as hard as iron. "If Petunia is here, she'll need someone to look out for her while you deal with Mrs. Bateman."

He couldn't argue that. "Come on then, but stay behind me."

He thought she might protest further, but she slipped into his shadow and they set out.

The inn was darkly paneled, with low ceilings. Matthew felt as if they'd entered a cave. A chubby fellow swathed in a white apron hurried up to them, but he took one look at Matthew's battered face and started shaking his head. "We don't take kindly to fights here, my lad."

"Then tell me where Mrs. Bateman is staying, and you'll

have no trouble from me," Matthew promised.

Again he shook his shaggy head. "Why should I trouble a customer?"

Charlotte stepped around Matthew. "Please, sir. A young girl's life may be at stake."

He looked Charlotte up and down, then straightened. "Room 12. Up the stairs and to your left. Be careful. She's already taken her ire out on two of the maids."

Charlotte shuddered.

Matthew led the way up the narrow stairs, footsteps sounding unnaturally loud. He located the room along the white-plastered corridor and opened the door before Charlotte could knock.

Mrs. Bateman was seated by the fire, shoes off and stockinged toes pointed toward the warmth. She tipped her chin at him. "What are you doing here?"

"Where's Petunia?" Matthew demanded, striding into the room.

She shrugged. "How should I know?"

He pulled up beside her chair. "Don't tell me you're innocent."

She shifted on the seat. "All right. I tried for a visit. You were out beating up another poor fellow, so I thought, what's the harm in trying? I saw her leave the house with that monster of a dog." She hitched her shawl closer. "He tried to take a bite out of me. You should put him down."

"I'll reward him for his trouble," Matthew said. "After you tell me what you did with Tuny."

"Nothing. Brat wanted no more to do with me. That's your fault. Poisoning her mind. And you." She pointed at Charlotte in the doorway. "Putting ideas in her head."

"I will ask you one more time," Matthew gritted out, "and then I will call the constable. Where is Petunia?"

She glanced between the two of them, face turning

ashen. "You really don't know? She ran off with the dog when I tried to take her with me. I thought she'd gone home. If she's really missing, you must find her!"

CHAPTER TWENTY-ONE

Charlotte wasn't sure she could believe Matthew's stepmother, but the woman was right about one thing. They had to find Petunia. London had never been a kind place for a girl on her own. Charlotte was just thankful the summer days were long. They still had hours before night fell.

"Where's Tuny?" Ivy begged when Matthew handed Charlotte into the coach in the innyard.

"Not here," Charlotte explained. "Mrs. Bateman claims your sister ran off when she attempted to convince Petunia to come with her."

Ivy's face fell. "Then we drove all this way for nothing."

Lord Kendall's hand covered hers a moment before withdrawing.

"Not necessarily," Matthew said as he and Charlotte took their seats. "We know she isn't here, and she was last seen not far from the house." He turned to Lord Kendall. "My lord, would you return us home?"

"Of course," Lord Kendall said. He called to his coachman, and the carriage set out once more.

Charlotte's mind was busy. "We'll need help. Miss Thorn would be glad to assist, I'm sure, and Worth, Lydia, and their staff."

Matthew's mouth quirked. "Building an army, are you?"

"Whatever it takes," Charlotte told him.

"You may count on my assistance as well," Lord Kendall put in. "My staff in London is small, but they are at your disposal."

Ivy smiled her gratitude.

The plan agreed, Matthew and Ivy alighted at the house. Charlotte waited only long enough to confirm that Petunia hadn't returned, then directed Lord Kendall's coachman to Clarendon Square. As she had suspected, her brother and his wife were glad to help. Worth had declined the prince's offer to celebrate Matthew's victory.

"Though we are short-staffed at present," her energetic sister-in-law confirmed. "Most of our servants aren't back yet from the holiday we gave them following the wedding. We only returned last night, and then Worth heard about this fight and there you are."

Charlotte assigned them to the streets to the north of Covent Garden and advised them where to check in every hour.

"Your organization is impressive," Lord Kendall said as they headed down the square to Meredith's townhouse.

"Most women who manage a household could do as well," Charlotte said. "Look at Ivy."

He nodded thoughtfully.

Meredith was eager to help, enlisting her servants and one other.

"We'll bring Fortune," she said, securing a leash to the jeweled collar on cat's neck. "Rufus may well catch her scent and pull Miss Petunia right to us."

Charlotte agreed. She assigned Miss Thorn's staff to the streets to the west of Covent Garden, then told them where to check in. She took her benefactress and Fortune into the carriage with Lord Kendall.

His face was neutral as he regarded the cat. Fortune stared back at him, copper-colored eyes unblinking.

"Miss Thorn," Charlotte said, "may I introduce Lord Kendall? He is a friend of Miss Bateman's who kindly agreed to assist us."

Meredith inclined her head. "My lord."

He nodded in return. "Miss Thorn. I've heard your name associated with the Duchess of Wey, Countess of Carrolton, and Lady Worthington. A matchmaker, I believe."

Meredith smiled. "Something of that sort." She glanced down at the grey-haired cat. "And this is Fortune. Fortune, say good-day to Lord Kendall." She eased her hold.

Fortune regarded his lordship a moment more, then turned her back and began washing one white-tipped paw.

Charlotte wasn't sure why, but disappointment bit at her. Meredith looked more disapproving, mouth tightening and raven brows dipping.

"The cut direct," Lord Kendall mused. "I must beg her pardon."

"Perhaps," Meredith said, transferring her frown to her pet.

He directed his driver to his home. Charlotte wasn't surprised to find a tall white-fronted townhouse with black shutters and wrought-iron trim, as traditional and upright as its owner. Lord Kendall went into the house and returned with two footmen and a groom, who climbed up at the back and top of the coach for the trip to the Bateman home.

Ivy must have been watching for them, for she hurried out as they pulled up.

Charlotte lowered the window. "Has she been found?"

"No," Ivy said, pausing to catch her breath. "Matthew, Daisy, and Betsy searched around the house again and could find no trace. Mr. Winthrop says he hasn't seen her or Rufus."

Charlotte nodded. "Very well then. You and Daisy go with Lord Kendall and his staff and search the streets to the south. Miss Thorn and I will go with Matthew to the eastern quarter. We have teams canvasing the north and west. We will all report back at the top of every hour. We will find her."

They regrouped and set out, Fortune scampering along on the leash. Every few minutes she shrugged or rubbed her face against Meredith's lavender skirts as if protesting the confinement. Matthew looked just as uncomfortable. His eyes were narrowed and focused, as if he faced an opponent greater than Lord Harding. Against the pallor of his skin, his bruises blazed a path of color. Charlotte hurt for him.

And she began to fear for Petunia. The girl was clever and spry. If she had not found her way home, something must be wrong.

Matthew called her name every few feet, to the annoyance of those on the street. One look his way was generally enough to send them hurrying about their business. Meredith kept bending over Fortune and murmuring low, as if asking the cat's advice. Fortune stayed close, gaze darting about as if she wasn't sure of her surroundings.

Neither was Charlotte. They had gone through the piazza, wandered around most of the closer streets, and crossed Drury Lane with all its traffic. The lorries, horses, and carriages pressed close together, moving faster than safety dictated. She shuddered to think of Petunia and Rufus navigating that busy thoroughfare. Now the houses and shops were packed so tightly that no sunlight trickled onto the street between. The sound of traffic faded, until all that could be heard was a shout of a man in anger, the cry of a lonely babe.

How frightened Petunia must be. Charlotte was frightened for her. She caught herself edging closer to Matthew. He took her hand, held it tight, and the darkness eased.

"Fortune?" Meredith asked.

The cat had stopped before an alley, back arching. Her hiss of warning echoed in the still darkness.

Not as loud as the bay of the hound in answer.

"Keep the cat back," Matthew advised before dropping Charlotte's hand and barging into the shaded crevice. "Petunia!" he shouted. "Tuny!"

"M-M-Matty?"

The stuttering voice pierced Charlotte's heart, and she paced Matthew as he broke into a run.

In the dubious shelter of a boarded-up doorway, Petunia sat on the crumbling brick stoop with Rufus leaning heavily against her dirty skirts. The hound rose and ambled to meet Matthew, tail wagging. Matthew took his collar and led him back to Petunia.

Tears streaked through the dust on the girl's face as he knelt beside her. "Oh, Matty, you found us."

Charlotte wanted to reach out, gather her close, but she knew it wasn't her place. She watched as Matthew brushed the hair off his sister's forehead.

"What happened, Sweet Pea?" he murmured.

She sniffed. "I was taking Rufus for a walk when I spotted a hired coach following us. Daisy says they look for girls to steal and sell to Scotland."

Charlotte made a note to speak to Daisy.

"I started walking faster, and the coach stopped, and there was Mrs. Bateman." She sniffed again. "She wanted me to come with her, but I knew you wouldn't like that, Matty. And I want to stay with you. So, I ran away from her. Rufus liked running so well he didn't want to stop. He got away from me. When I finally caught him, I wasn't sure where I was. And I fell along the way."

She twitched her skirts aside to reveal a knee purple and swollen. "It hurts something awful to walk. I'm sorry, Matty."

He gathered her close. "You have no reason to apologize, Sweet Pea. You did what you could to keep you and Rufus safe. I'm proud of you. Now, let's get you home and cleaned up." He lifted her against his chest.

Petunia rested her head against his shoulder. "I knew

you'd come, Matty. You always take care of us."

Tears burned Charlotte's eyes as Matthew carried his sister past her, Rufus' leash trailing from the girl's fingers. He walked slowly enough that the old dog could keep pace. When Charlotte didn't follow immediately, he stopped and waited until she joined them, his smile relieved and thankful.

Why had she doubted him? This was the real Matthew Bateman—loving brother, considerate friend. She had attempted to mold him into a gentleman, but he had had the heart and character all along. Small wonder she'd fallen in love with him.

She bit her lip to keep from saying the words aloud as they exited the alley. Against the rules, against her dubious plans for her future, against the hurt of her past, she had given him her heart. She had felt the wall between them. Why hadn't she realized she'd help build it? Her father, Worth, and John Curtis had been unreliable, so she had determined to rely on no one but herself. She might have continued that lonely existence if not for Matthew and his sisters. He was a man she could count on. She could scarcely breathe at the enormity of it.

Which was just as well. Now was not the time to confess her devotion. Now they needed to get Petunia home and into a physician's care.

Rufus had other ideas. He must have caught Fortune's scent, for he set up a howl and started forward, nearly tugging Petunia out of Matthew's arms. Charlotte rescued the leash and pulled him to a stop before he could do more than snuff at the cat, who was leaning back and eyeing him with considerable disdain.

"That is quite enough," Meredith informed him, and he quieted, dropping his head sheepishly. Fortune batted his nose as if to reassert her position as mistress.

Charlotte felt as humbled as the hound. She'd always admired Matthew, but her feelings had grown beyond what she would have thought possible.

Still, the only way to know whether he returned those feelings was to ask.

Matthew stood beside Tuny's bed two hours later, watching the gentle rise and fall of her chest. He'd never been so thankful as the moment he'd found her safe, but he hadn't been able to relax until the physician had seen her.

"Her knee is badly twisted," the older man told Matthew, Ivy, Daisy, and Charlotte as they gathered in the little bedchamber. "But not broken. I'll leave laudanum for the pain in case she needs it. You know about poultices?"

Ivy nodded. "Perhaps lavender?"

"Excellent thought. Make sure she says in bed for the next few days until the swelling goes down. I'll stop by tomorrow to check on her."

Matthew saw him to the door. It was the least he could do. Charlotte had alerted the other searchers, sent for the physician, and thanked her brother, Lord Kendall, and Miss Thorn for their trouble before sending them on their way. All his focus had been on his sister.

"Do you need something for your injuries?" the physician asked. "I heard you beat Harding, but he seems to have landed a few blows if that purple eye is any indication."

He'd forgotten about the injuries from the fight. The aches rushed at him now, demanding attention. They would have to wait.

"They're nothing serious," Matthew told him. "I've had enough broken bones to know. I'll have Ivy make me a poultice too. But thank you." He shut the door behind the fellow.

Upstairs came the sound of Daisy's laugh, Charlotte's reply. Nothing would have made him happier than to join them, but he had one more duty to perform before the day was out.

"Tell them I'll be back shortly," he said to Betsy, who was heading up the stairs with a tray of tea and biscuits. Then he let himself out.

The innkeeper gave him no trouble this time as Matthew headed for his stepmother's room. He did her the courtesy of knocking and entered when she called permission. Her bags were open on the floor, and she was halfway between them and the wardrobe, clothing draped over her arms.

"Did you find her?" she demanded.

Matthew nodded. "Twisted her knee, but otherwise fine. Are you leaving?"

She dropped the clothing in the bag and bent to shove them in. "Tomorrow."

Matthew crossed his arms over his chest. "Why? I thought you were determined to wring money from me one way or another."

She curled her lip as she straightened. "And you were a disappointment there too. Got what I could from the gossip sheets for my story. I thought you'd win a fine purse, fighting for the prince, but the papers said it was all for fun." She sneered. "Stupid waste."

He wasn't sure whether she meant the lack of money or her time. "It wouldn't have mattered," he told her. "You'll get no more from me. Ever. If you try to make trouble again, I'll see you up on charges."

"Charges?" She shook her head. "Who do you think they'll believe, the poor widow or the Beast of Birmingham?"

"Or Sir Matthew Bateman," he countered. "Friend of Viscount Worthington and the Earl of Carrolton."

She stilled, jaw moving as if she chewed on the idea. Then she made a show of shrugging. "It's of no account in any event. I met a fellow while I was here. He's interested in becoming better acquainted."

Matthew pitied him. "Where's he from?"

She tossed her head. "Ireland. He says if I come home with him, he'll treat me like a queen. So, you'll no more have the pleasure of my company, and don't ask for favors, for I won't grant them."

Matthew spread his hands. "May Ireland be exactly what you deserve."

"It will be," she insisted. "Now, get out. I have packing to be done. Tell that innkeeper I expect a maid to help." She rubbed her hands together. "A queen, says he."

Matthew turned away. Only time would tell if she was truly out of their lives, but he knew of only one lady who deserved to be treated like a queen.

Would she be willing to settle for being the wife of a knight?

CHAPTER TWENTY-TWO

Tuny woke the next morning ready to go. Ivy enlisted Matthew in dissuading her.

"But I'm fine," his littlest sister protested, tugging at the covers, while Daisy sat, holding them in place. "Rufus needs to go for a walk."

The hound let out a snore and rolled onto his back on the rug.

"If Rufus needs exercise, I'll take him," Matthew promised. "But you're staying in bed until the physician says otherwise."

Tuny pouted. "What's he know, anyway?"

"More than you," Daisy said, tucking her muslin skirts more firmly around her legs as if intending to stay a while.

"Know-it-all," Tuny complained.

"Brat," Daisy countered. Then she grinned. "It's good to have you home."

Tuny beamed.

"I'll make you a bargain," Matthew said, leaning closer to the girl. "You promise to stay in bed and mind Ivy and Daisy, and I'll let you in on a secret."

Tuny's eyes narrowed. "What kind of secret?"

"You won't know unless you promise."

Tuny leaned back against the headboard. "I promise to stay in bed—"

"And mind your sisters," Daisy prompted her.

"And mind my sisters," she agreed, "so long as you tell me a secret worth my while."

He wouldn't get better than that. And if Tuny didn't think his plan was worthwhile, he had no chance of convincing Charlotte.

"Agreed," he said. He lowered his voice. "I'm heading over to see Lord Worthington and ask for Charlotte's hand."

Daisy squealed, then clapped her hands over her mouth. Her eyes still sparkled over the top of her fingers.

"Why'd you need his permission?" Tuny asked. "You're a knight. He's just an old viscount."

Daisy dropped her hands. "Viscounts are better than knights, silly. And that's what gentlemen do when they propose to a lady, request permission from the head of the family. Remember what Charlotte told us? She doesn't have a father, so Matty has to ask her brother."

"If I ever have a beau, he better talk to me first," Tuny grumbled.

Matty glanced between them. "Have I got it wrong, then?"

"No," Daisy said with a scowl at her sister. "You ask Lord Worthington, and then you ask Charlotte. It's what a lady would expect."

Tuny humphed. "All right. And that was a very good secret, Matty. I'll stay put. Just see that you tell me what she says."

"What he says," Daisy corrected her.

"I don't care about him," Tuny insisted. "All that matters is what Charlotte says."

Matthew knew she was right. But Charlotte was used to proper forms, polite manners, and he wanted to show her he understood. Accordingly, he dressed in his best suit, the one he'd worn at his elevation, had Ivy help him tie a credible knot in his cravat, and took himself over to the Worthington townhouse.

The blond-haired maid who answered his knock at the

door smiled at him. "What you doin' knockin', Beast? You could have come 'round the kitchen. We'd have let you right in. You're a hero, you are, giving that old Lord Harding what's what."

Matthew stepped into the familiar entryway. How many times had he passed that painting of a ship in full sail? Like it, he had gone nowhere until he'd met Charlotte and her brother. Now the light-blue walls seemed taller, the corridor stretching to the back of the house and the withdrawing room longer. And he had never quite looked so pale as his reflection showed in the oval, gilt-framed mirror beside the door.

Matthew turned away from the glass and squared his shoulders. "I've come to see his lordship, Katie."

"He's in the rear garden on the right side," she said. "Workin' on that balloon of his. Will you be comin' back into service here, then?"

"No," Matthew told her. "I have other plans."

She sighed. "Pity. You know the way."

He'd followed it often enough. Lord Worthington had bought the townhouse next door and broken through the walls in places. He used the other house for his scientific studies. Matthew walked the corridor and turned for the doorway into the other house. The floor sloped down slightly. He followed it to the door to the rear garden, where the man he had come to consider a friend was bent over a massive strip of scarlet silk.

"Still improving, I see," Matthew ventured.

Worth looked up with a smile. A tall, slender man with hair as russet as his sister's, his eyes always looked more silver than grey to Matthew, as if something gleamed inside.

"Always," he said. "The balloon requires a way to be lowered in altitude without actually landing. The French use a flap near the top of the envelope, but the control mechanisms are unreliable. I'm trying to find an alternative."

Matthew cocked a smile. "So, you took all the trouble

to stitch that envelope, and now you want to poke a hole in it."

Worth grinned. "That's the idea." He lowered the silk. "Good to see you, Bateman. You just missed Lydia. She's off to visit her brother. Lend me a hand?"

Matthew wasn't sure what he needed, but he followed him to where a bronze brazier stood smoking on a cork pedestal. Matthew peered through the heat. "What are you burning now?"

"Peat," Worth admitted. "I know, I know, we'd ruled it out initially. But I've found that once it starts burning, it keeps burning for an admirable amount of time. There is an issue of weight, however. Lift that and see what you think."

A shovel stuck out of a high box full of haphazardly-piled cut peat. Mindful of his fancy suit, Matthew pulled up the shovel, slid it under a mat of the woody material, and lifted.

"Heavier than the same amount of coal," he admitted. "And you had some trouble with managing that weight, I recall."

"Hm, yes." Worth took a pair of iron tongs and rearranged the peat in the brazier, then nodded to Matthew to add more. The brazier moaned with the weight.

"Definitely a consideration," Worth said. "Was there a reason you called?"

The shovel slid from his fingers to clunk against the ground, and the words dried up in his mouth. Worth didn't appear to notice, taking out his chronometer to consult the time. How did a knight beg a viscount to be allowed to join their families? Was there some form he should be using? Some handshake that eluded him?

Matthew straightened. He had no call for concern. Lord Worthington had treated him well before the gulf in their stations had been narrowed. Matthew had never minced words with him before. He shouldn't start now.

"I love your sister," he said. "And I'd like your permission to ask her to marry me."

"Certainly," Worth said, eyeing the peat. "Let me try the shovel."

Matthew stepped aside as Worth bent over the pile of peat. "Did you even hear what I said?"

"Of course." Worth scooped up a mat and bobbed it up and down as if weighing it. "You'd like to marry Charlotte. I think it a fine idea."

It couldn't be that easy. "Why?" Matthew asked with a frown. "A knight is still below a viscount. I'm not wealthy. Some won't receive her because she's my wife."

"All facts that have no bearing on the matter." Worth dropped the peat back into the pile.

"How do you figure?" Matthew demanded.

Worth straightened and ticked off the reasons on his fingers. "A title has never been important to Charlotte. She has a small inheritance—the two of you should get by just fine. And a great many ladies stopped receiving her when she refused to wed and began helping me. Her true friends didn't desert then, and they won't now. Besides, my sister loves you."

Matthew had to sit down, hitting the box of peat with a thump that shook the pile. "She told you that?"

"She didn't have to," Worth replied. "She is happiest in your presence. I saw that even before I married Lydia. That, sir, is love." He nodded as if satisfied with both his work and his argument.

Matthew rose, still not sure he could believe the tale. "I suppose I should ask her, then."

"I suppose you should." Worth's grin reappeared. "Cheer up, Matthew. Marriage is nothing like one of your fights. It's bold and brave and beautiful, and it will leave you a better man."

Matthew could only hope he was right, about Charlotte's feelings especially.

Charlotte climbed the steps to the Bateman home. This was likely the last time she would do so as an etiquette teacher. Anyone could see that her work here was done. Ivy and Daisy were receiving invitations on their own, and Matthew could escort them to any events. Besides, she suspected Lord Kendall would soon propose. Matthew had survived his elevation and was well on his way toward being respected by those with more open minds. It was time to decide what to do next with her life.

And whether she could convince Matthew to be a part of it.

The maid answered her knock, but Ivy stepped out of the sitting room and swept up to them.

"I'll see to Miss Worthington, Betsy," she told the maid, who curtsied and went about her business.

"How is Petunia?" Charlotte asked.

"Much better," Ivy told her with a smile. "The physician thinks she may be able to rise sooner than he had hoped."

"That's good news."

"Not good enough for Tuny. She wants up now. Daisy is with her, but I should take my turn. Matthew is expecting you. Go right up."

Charlotte nodded and started up the stairs. She was aware that Ivy was watching. As she paused on the landing, another door cracked open, and she caught sight of Daisy and Petunia. From the bed, Petunia gave her two thumbs up.

Odd. She'd almost think she was here to accept a position, not terminate one.

Matthew was standing by the fire when she entered. Ah, the elevation suit. How well he looked in it, so tall, broad shoulders showing to advantage. And who had tied that cravat? The elegant swath of white brought out the tan of his face, the dark of his eyes.

"Charlotte," he greeted her, looking nearly as solemn as Lord Kendall. "Won't you have a seat?"

Nerves tingling, she went to take her usual chair, and he sat opposite her. His gaze swept over her, as if searching for something. She patted her lacy green skirts into place.

"I understand Petunia is doing well," she ventured when the silence stretched.

He managed a tight smile. "Already giving us orders."

Silence fell once more, the stillness broken only by the shift of his muscular body in the chair. Charlotte took a deep breath. She had rehearsed her speech several times and knew just how she meant to approach the matter.

"Matthew, I must thank you for allowing me to tutor your sisters and to advise you. I enjoy your family so much. I realize you no longer have need of my services, but I want you to know I will always care about you."

"All of us?" The interruption was almost a challenge.

She swallowed. "Yes, of course. Ivy, Daisy, Petunia, even Rufus."

"And me?"

This was the hardest part. "Yes. And you, Matthew. You most of all." There was more. She knew she'd had more, but something lit in his eyes and she could not find the words. Slowly, carefully, as if expecting a protest any moment, he went down on one knee before her.

"And I will always care about you, Charlotte. You bring light and hope and order everywhere you go. I saw that in your brother's house, and I see it here. You gave me a glimpse of what it truly means to be a family, the sort I'd always dreamed of, with a husband and wife who love and respect each other, who work together for the good of their family. I know I don't have much to offer you—no fortune, little consequence—but if you'd ever consider—that is…"

Charlotte stared at him, joy and doubt battling inside her. "Are you asking me to marry you?"

"Yes?" he said as if the same forces fought inside him.

"Then yes. Today, tomorrow, as soon as you can procure a special license. I love you, Matthew, and—"

Whatever great speech she'd planned was swept away as he surged to his feet, pulled her up and into his embrace, and kissed her. The touch carried her beyond rules, beyond expectations, beyond her carefully constructed wall, into a future led by love. Here—at this house, with this family, in his arms—was where she belonged.

She wasn't sure how long it had been when he released her. The grin on his face brightened the room.

"Special license, eh?" he asked. "Can knights request one of those?"

"From the Archbishop," Charlotte said. She reached up and caressed a lock of hair off his forehead.

He caught her hand, held it in his own. "I love you, Charlotte. I have for some time, but I never thought you'd consider me. I may not be able to give you the jewels and fine carriages you deserve, but I will be the best husband a lady could want."

"And I plan on being the best wife a knight could ask," Charlotte said. "But we won't be poor, Matthew. My mother left me an inheritance."

His scowl threatened. "I won't take your money."

"You will if you love me," she countered. "I want to contribute to our home too. And Ivy and Daisy will need dowries. And when Tuny is older, we'll need to bring her out properly."

Matthew's scowl disappeared, and he pulled her close once more. "What would I do without you?"

"Kneel to a knight when you have no need to kneel to anyone," Charlotte said, warm in his arms. "Now, let's go tell the girls. I have a feeling they're expecting good news, and I wouldn't want to disappoint my new sisters."

CHAPTER TWENTY-THREE

She should find another client.

Meredith sat on the sofa in her withdrawing room, stroking Fortune's coat and smiling to herself. Charlotte was upstairs packing her things, having brought the news that she was engaged to be married to Sir Matthew. They planned to wed in the next few days. How delightful.

Her smile slipped. Yes, delightful for Charlotte, but for the first time, Meredith was at a loss. Mr. Cowls had offered no other insights as to gently reared ladies who found themselves in need of a position. Nor had she met any likely candidates herself. Her last few clients had simply walked through the door.

Fortune stiffened a moment before the knock sounded downstairs.

Meredith laughed. "Perfect timing, perhaps?"

Mr. Cowls led up Lord Kendall.

Meredith hid her surprise as the slender lord inclined his head in greeting. "My lord, to what do I owe this pleasure?"

He flipped up the tails on his dove grey morning coat and seated himself on the chair across from her. "I had two reasons for calling. One was to make amends to your pet."

Meredith glanced down at Fortune, whose tail swished lazily back and forth against the sofa. Her copper-colored eyes were half closed, as if his lordship's company already bored her.

"Fortune is discriminating in her opinions," Meredith allowed. "I cannot imagine why she would take you in dislike." She raised her head to eye him.

He shifted on the chair as if the very idea made him uncomfortable. "I have been told animals can sense temperament. I have perhaps been more melancholy in the last year, though I try to hide it."

Fortune did not care for half-truths, Meredith had found. Perhaps she had felt something hesitant about the marquess that indicated his lie.

"My condolences, my lord," she told him. "Lady Kendall was far too young to leave us."

His sad smile agreed with her.

"And how is your daughter?" she asked.

He did not brighten. Indeed, she felt as if the room was darkening. "I am told she struggles to thrive. Which brings me to my second reason for calling."

"Oh?" Meredith prompted, curious despite herself.

He touched one corner of his mustache, as if the topic he meant to pursue was of only minor interest. "You found unconventional brides for Carrolton, Worthington, the Duke of Wey, and, I'm told, Sir Harold Orwell. I find myself in need of a similar sort of bride."

Meredith eyed him. His face was noncommittal, his smile pleasant. Where was the anticipation, the eagerness any bride might hope to see in her groom?

"You are a marquess of good family with a sound fortune," she pointed out. "Your options would seem endless."

He grimaced. "Some ladies of the *ton* might expect more than I am capable of giving. They might also believe it inconvenient to mother another woman's child."

"Ah," Meredith said. "What you want is a nanny."

"I have a nanny," he clipped out. "The second in the last seven months. Neither was able to give Sophia the devotion she needs to grow. I will not lose her."

She had thought him dispassionate. She had been wrong.

His despair welled up inside him, spilled past the neat mustache, the unassuming smile. His loss weighed upon him, and he feared for his child. He needed her help perhaps more than any client who had graced her door.

As if she agreed, Fortune rose and leaped to his lap to lay her head against his chest.

Brows rising in obvious surprise, he ran his gloved hand gently along her back. "Well, at least I achieved one of my objectives."

"And I fear I cannot help you with the other," Meredith said, not without a touch of sadness herself. "I place gentlewomen in need of positions, my lord. It is merely a coincidence that they have gone on to marry within the house."

Fortune leaned away to look up at him, for all the world as if grinning.

A smile tugged at his mouth as he gazed down at her. "Coincidence. I see." He looked up at Meredith. "May I ask you to give the matter some thought? Perhaps you can find some lady who would be willing to take the position of mother to my child."

Meredith shook her head. "A nanny is a position. A wife is not. What you want, sir, is a wife."

"And so do I."

Meredith blinked at Julian standing in the doorway. His arms were akimbo, widening the shoulders of his navy coat. His eyes were narrowed on the marquess seated across from her.

Lord Kendall swiveled to see who had spoken.

"Forgive the interruption," Julian said, striding into the room with a nod to the marquess. "Mr. Cowls did not tell me Miss Thorn was entertaining, and I didn't see a carriage outside."

"I left my carriage down the way," Lord Kendall explained.

Why? Was he ashamed of what he was doing? The

marquess certainly held his feelings deep, and only Fortune had realized the polite smile was merely a façade.

The marquess set Fortune down and climbed to his feet. "I have taken enough of your time, Miss Thorn. I do hope you will consider my request."

Once more all polish and no emotion. She wanted so much to help him, but she could not, in good conscience, place a lady as a "wife" in name only. She had never appreciated marriages of convenience.

"I will send word if I think of a lady who meets your requirements, my lord," Meredith said.

Fortune walked him out. Julian stepped aside to let them pass, then came to sit beside Meredith on the sofa.

"Looking for a wife, eh?" he asked. "Have I been misplaced?"

"Never," Meredith assured him. "Thank you for rescuing me. I wasn't sure what else to say to the fellow. He seems to have taken me for a matchmaker."

Julian smiled. "Perhaps it's time you realized you and Fortune are matchmakers. Four positions, four brides."

"Five," Meredith said. "Charlotte Worthington is to marry Sir Matthew."

Julian whistled. "Now, that's a match."

"I think they will be good for each other," Meredith said with justifiable pride.

"And you are good for me," Julian said. "Might I hope you feel the same way?"

Meredith laughed. "Certainly sir. I think Fortune and I have been the making of you."

He didn't smile at her tease, gaze determined. "You have. Ever since Eton, I have done all I could to advance. Once I thought it was to establish myself, so we could marry."

"I remember," Meredith said, the old hurt crawling over her again. "You were so certain we must wait until you could better afford a wife. And then we were parted."

"And then we were parted." He took her hand. "You

understand now that I searched for you but had no way of knowing what had become of you. The few times you were in London with Lady Winhaven, I was working. But even without you at my side, the need to advance didn't ease. I have curried favor with the most prestigious houses, done things that shame me now. I told myself it would be worth the trouble if I earned the respect I craved. I was wrong."

He had always been able to put her at a loss for words. Meredith lay her free hand over his. "You had no need to strive so hard. You won my respect, the respect of your friends, ages ago."

"I have come to see that," he said, gaze on their joined hands. "But more than that, Meredith, I have come to realize there is one person whose opinion truly matters. Yours."

Meredith trembled. "You know I love you, Julian. I have since I was a girl."

"And I love you, my darling Meredith." He released her to slip off the sofa and onto one knee, gaze holding hers. "That's why I must speak. Ten years ago, you asked me what you could do to elicit a proposal. I have regretted my answer ever since. So, I ask you: what can I do now to convince you to be my bride?"

She had waited so long, doubted so often. The answer was easy.

"Nothing," she said. "I need no convincing. I would be delighted to marry you, Julian."

He rose and pulled her up and into his arms. As his head bent to hers, her heart started beating faster. Then something brushed her skirts: Fortune, returned from escorting Lord Kendall.

Julian must have felt the movement too, for he stepped back and looked down. "Ah, I see my mistake. Fortune, may I have the honor of marrying your mistress?"

Fortune curled around his legs, purring. Then she

bumped the back of his calves as if urging him closer to Meredith.

With a laugh, he pulled Meredith close and kissed her.

This was joy, this was love. This was what they had both longed for all these years. Finally, finally, he had returned to her, and she would never let him go again.

Perhaps Fortune truly was a matchmaker at heart.

Who would her pet find for the marquess?

Dear Reader

Thank you for choosing Charlotte and Matthew's story. They were perfect for each other, but it took a while for each to settle their pasts and realize it. If you missed their introduction to the Fortune's Brides series, look for *Never Vie for a Viscount*.

If you enjoyed this book, there are several things you could do now:

Sign up for a free e-mail alert at my website at *www.reginascott.com* so you'll be the first to know whenever a new book is out or on sale. I offer exclusive free short stories to my subscribers from time to time. Don't miss out.

Post a review on a bookseller site or Goodreads to help others find the book.

Turn the page for a sneak peek of the sixth book in the series, *Never Marry a Marquess*, in which Ivy Bateman becomes the prime candidate for Lord Kendall's next wife. Can the sweet, gentle Ivy prove to the weary widower that love, and a good cinnamon bun, truly can heal all wounds?

Blessings!

Regina Scott

Sneak Peek
NEVER MARRY A MARQUESS
Book 6 in the Fortune's Brides Series by Regina Scott

London, England, July 1812

Would she ever become accustomed to Society?
Sitting in the hired coach, Ivy Bateman smoothed down the satin skirts of her evening gown, the color reminding her of clotted cream. Since her brother Matthew had been elevated to a hereditary knighthood for saving the prince's life, her life had changed. Where once she had spent her days keeping his house and caring for her younger sisters, now she entertained fine ladies over tea and promenaded in Hyde Park at the fashionable hour. In the evenings, she used to read a thrilling adventure novel by the fire before taking her weary body off to bed to dream. Now she sometimes didn't reach her bed before the sun rose. And she found herself dreaming of things she was not meant to have.

"Stay by my side at the soiree," Miss Thorn advised

from across the coach. "I will ensure we only converse with gentlemen Charlotte or your brother have already approved."

Ivy's younger sister, Daisy, shifted beside her, her pale pink gown whispering against the padded leather seat. "That's no fun. What if a charming prince asks for an introduction? I'm expected to turn my back on him?"

"Alas, princes, charming or otherwise, are in short supply, even for the earl and countess." Miss Thorn adjusted her long silk gloves. "And any fellow who approaches without an introduction cannot be a gentleman."

Daisy slumped, then perked up again. "But if you were to introduce him to us, that would be permissible? We can't help that Charlotte and Matthew are out of town."

Their brother and his bride were off on their honeymoon to the Lakes District. A shame Ivy couldn't have gone along, if only to escape the hubbub that was London as the Season wound to a close. But Matthew and Charlotte deserved time to themselves. Miss Thorn, who had introduced Charlotte into the Bateman household as an etiquette teacher, had offered to serve as chaperone in Charlotte's absence so Ivy and Daisy could continue the social whirl.

Miss Thorn probably didn't worry that her hair was piled up properly or her gown was too simple. The lavender silk with its rows of pleats at the hem was the exact shade of her eyes. Not a curl of her raven hair escaped the pearl-studded combs that held it in place. Still, the employment agency owner looked odd without her cat Fortune in her arms.

"I expect to know a number of the attendees," Miss Thorn allowed, and Daisy brightened, until she continued. "Most will be at least a decade older than you and happily married. But if I spot a likely gentleman, I will be sure to draw his attention. Just see that you ask him to call so that Fortune may give her blessing."

Fortune had an uncanny way of knowing whether a person was worthwhile. And to think she approved of Ivy.

The cat had been less approving of her sister, and Ivy couldn't help wondering if Daisy's impetuous nature wasn't to blame.

Now her sister puffed out a sigh. "Old people shouldn't be allowed to host events."

Ivy put a hand on her arm. "A decade older than sixteen is not so very aged. Besides, you know Lady Carrolton will host a lovely soiree in her new home. Remember her ball?"

"Yes," Daisy said. "But she's just a countess, and a French one at that. Matthew is friends with the prince. We should be moving in higher circles."

"This is quite high enough for me," Ivy assured her.

Daisy turned her gaze out the window.

Ivy caught herself smoothing her skirts again and forced her gloved hands to stop. She might feel uncomfortable in such glittering company as the earl and his wife, but Daisy only wanted more. At times, she reminded Ivy of their stepmother.

She must fight any connection there. Mrs. Bateman was easily the most grasping, the cruelest woman Ivy had ever met. Last they had heard, she had taken up with a wealthy Irishman and headed across the sea to his country. Ivy could only hope they never saw her again.

Miss Thorn gathered her fan. "Here we are now. Stay beside me, girls. We wouldn't want to be separated in the crush."

"*You* wouldn't want us to be separated," Daisy muttered.

Oh no. Ivy had been both mother and sister since she was twelve. She was not about to let Daisy slip away. She linked arms with her sister as soon as they alighted.

At times, she marveled at the differences between them. Ivy was tall and curvy. Daisy was a pocket Venus, the same curves poured into a much shorter stature. Ivy's hair was a sunny blond like their mother's, Daisy's a thick dark brown like their brother's and father's. The one thing they shared was a pair of walnut-colored eyes, but while Ivy tended to look at the world in wonder, Daisy viewed it in calculation.

But they both stared up at the house they were about to enter.

The Earl of Carrolton had owned a London townhouse not far from Miss Thorn's on Clarendon Square. To honor his bride, he'd recently purchased and had renovated a larger house set off the square with its own gardens. Now the cream-colored stones glowed in the light of lanterns hung from the trees, and every window gleamed with candlelight.

"Beeswax," Daisy hissed to Ivy as they entered the marble-tiled hall and were directed up a set of sweeping stairs to the gallery. "You won't find an earl using tallow."

Indeed, no cost had been spared in decorating the house. The walls of the long gallery were covered in watered silk the radiant blue of the sky at sunrise, and oil paintings in gilded frames hung from the high ceilings. The teal and amber carpet sank under Ivy's satin slippers. She knew by the feel. She certainly couldn't see much of it, as the room was filled with London's finest, elbow to elbow, clustered in groups. Jewels flashed as ladies turned to greet friends. Laughter rode on the tide of conversation.

Daisy was craning her neck as Miss Thorn navigated them through the crowd. "I don't see Sir William." She had run into the rascal of a baronet more than once this Season and counted him a favorite. "But there are one or two fellows who might do."

"You may have them all," Ivy told her, stopping to allow Miss Thorn to speak to an old friend.

After they had been introduced and the two women were chatting, Daisy nudged Ivy. "Waiting for Lord Kendall, are we?"

The floor seemed to dip beneath Ivy's feet. "Of course

not. We don't even know whether he'll be in attendance."

Daisy shook her head. "You can't fool me, Ivy Bateman. You want to be a marquessa."

"Marchioness," Ivy corrected her, and her sister grinned.

Ivy didn't waste her breath arguing. Daisy was certain Ivy was smitten with the Marquess of Kendall. What lady wouldn't be? He was tall and elegantly formed, and he held himself as if he well knew his own worth. That sable hair curled back from a brow that spoke of intellect. His neat beard and mustache framed a mouth that offered compassion, suggested kindness. With a family as old as the Conquest and a fortune as deep as a well, he could easily have any lady he chose.

He would not choose her. Matthew might have been elevated, but Ivy was still the daughter of a millworker. She and Daisy were fortunate that their new sister-in-law, Charlotte, was the daughter of a viscount and sister to Lord Worthington, or they would likely never have set foot in a Society event. Even when they did, some refused to speak to them, gazed at them when they passed as if aghast someone so common would be allowed admittance.

Still, the Countess of Carrolton had invited them, and, as the evening wore on, Ivy did her best to honor the lady. She accompanied Miss Thorn as she made her way around the room, greeted acquaintances, chatted about the weather, the ridiculous war America had declared on her mother country, and the latest fashion. Daisy lagged behind or forged ahead from time to time, but Miss Thorn or Ivy always managed to pull her back into their circle. Ivy knew Miss Thorn was keeping an eye on Daisy, but after caring for her sister since they'd lost their mother, she found it difficult to remember she didn't have to be on her guard.

"Dare I claim this beauty for a promenade?" Sir William asked, gaze on Daisy and grin infectious.

Miss Thorn eyed him from his artfully curled blond hair to his polished evening pumps and inclined her head.

"Once around the room, sir. I will be watching."

He bowed, then offered Daisy his arm, and the pair set off, Daisy preening.

"She sets her sights high," Miss Thorn observed.

Unease pulled Ivy's shoulders tighter. "She's clever. She'll learn her place."

The employment agency owner transferred her gaze to Ivy. "And what place would that be?"

Ivy felt the need to step back and promptly bumped into another lady. Turning to apologize, she had to raise her chin to meet the fierce gaze of the Amazon standing there.

"I do beg your pardon, Mrs. Villers," Ivy said, dropping her chin.

"Miss Bateman," the lady intoned, sounding a bit as if she'd discovered a fly in her soup. "Miss Thorn."

"Mrs. Villers," Miss Thorn acknowledged. "Mr. Villers."

Ivy looked up in time to see the saturnine fellow at the lady's elbow raise a silver quizzing glass and examine Ivy and her chaperone through it.

"The Beast of Birmingham's sister, is it not?" he drawled.

"Sir Matthew Bateman's sister," Miss Thorn corrected him as Ivy's cheeks heated. "Miss Bateman, I don't believe you have met Mr. Villers. He is Lady Worthington's brother."

"And brother-in-law to the Earl of Carrolton," the fellow seemed compelled to remind her. "Good of you to come." He turned to his wife. "Isn't that dear Gregory waving us over, darling?" He offered his wife his arm, and the two sailed off, noses in the air.

"I do hope they don't go outside that way," Miss Thorn said. "If it was raining, they might drown."

Just then a footman approached them and bowed as well as he could among the crush. "I was asked to deliver this to you, miss." He offered Ivy a folded piece of parchment.

Ivy accepted it from him, mystified, then opened the note, aware of Miss Thorn's gaze on her.

I have made a cake of myself, the note read in Daisy's brisk hand. *Meet me in the library on the first floor, and don't bring Miss Thorn. I cannot face her now.*

"Trouble?" Miss Thorn asked.

Heart starting to beat faster, Ivy folded the note. "Just a friend reminding me of my duty. Will you excuse me? I won't be long."

Miss Thorn eyed her. Ivy willed her not to suggest she needed a chaperone, to remember they were at a party given by a trusted couple, to recall that Ivy was the reliable sister. Whether Miss Thorn heard Ivy's frantic thoughts or not, she inclined her head in consent, and Ivy hurried for the stairs.

The same footman directed her around the corner to the double doors of the library, and Ivy slipped inside. A single lamp had been left burning, leaving the corners in shadow. By its golden light, she made out tall oak cases, offering row upon row of books she would at another time have been delighted to peruse. Indeed, the deep leather sofa before the black marble hearth invited her to linger and read.

"Daisy?" Ivy called, venturing deeper into the room. "Miss Bateman?"

Ivy turned to find the Marquess of Kendall standing in the doorway. The black of his evening coat and breeches emphasized his height. The lamplight picked out gold in his sable hair. He shut the door behind him and moved closer. "How might I be of assistance?"

There must be some mistake. He should not be here. She should not be here. Ivy edged around the sofa, away from him. "I need no assistance, my lord. I was concerned for my sister."

He frowned, following her. "Your sister, Miss Daisy?"

"Yes." She rounded the other end of the sofa and started for the door. "I must have misunderstood. Excuse me." She seized the latch and tugged.

The door refused to open.

Stephen, Marquess of Kendall, watched as the pretty Miss Bateman pulled at the latch, color rising with each movement. She was such a cipher. The round face, the wide brown eyes, and her soft voice combined to make her appear sweet, uncertain, and full of amazement at the world. Yet there were moments when she exhibited an inner strength that surprised him. He had wondered whether she might be the woman he needed.

That woman had proven exceedingly difficult to find. Now that the Season was drawing to a close, his quest would become even more challenging. A marquess possessed of a decent fortune and an excellent family name ought to be able to locate a wife easily enough. But he didn't want a wife. He wanted a mother for Sophia.

Just the thought of his little daughter tightened his chest. Her mother had been the love of his life. It wasn't right that Adelaide had been taken so young, only the day after the birth of their daughter. Kendall never intended to give his heart again. How could he when it had gone to the grave with his wife?

But Sophia needed a mother, a woman who would cherish and guide her better than he could as her father. Oh, he knew not all mothers were so doting, but he had been assured his mother had been, that he would not be the man he was today without her love. And so he had come to London in search of a bride among the ladies on the marriage mart.

He'd soon realized his error. The ladies suited to be a marchioness fell into one of two camps. Either they were idealistic and hoped for a love match, or they delighted in Society and would never have enjoyed rusticating in Surrey and raising another woman's child. He had learned Miss Bateman had guided her younger sisters and loved children, but he doubted she'd be content in the type of marriage he intended to offer.

Now she stepped back from the door with a frown. "It appears to be stuck. Would you try, my lord?"

He offered her a polite smile and approached the door. Why was she dissembling? He'd received word from a footman that Miss Bateman requested his help on a matter of some urgency and would meet him in the library. He had not doubted the report. Since becoming acquainted with her family, he had been put in a position of offering assistance twice, most recently when her youngest sister had gone missing. That was the day he'd realized the strength inside her otherwise soft demeanor. Miss Bateman would have gone to the ends of the earth to see her sister safe.

Would that he found someone who cared so much about Sophia.

He took hold of the latch, gave it a good tug. Through the thick wood, he thought he heard a metallic rattle, but the door didn't budge.

"What's wrong?" Miss Bateman asked, fingers knitting before her creamy gown.

He yanked harder. Something creaked in protest, but still the door held firm. He released the handle and stepped back. "We appear to be trapped."

"How very inconvenient," she said.

Or was it convenient? He did not know her well, after all. Could she have set up this meeting to cry compromise? In the past, she had gone out of her way to avoid any situation that might be construed as intimate. Or did she, too, see her opportunities narrowing with the Season's end?

She could easily have taken advantage of the opportunity now. But she did not attempt to throw herself into his arms, begging for comfort in their circumstances. She went to sit on the sofa, back straight, head high. As he followed, he was not surprised to find her hands folded properly in her lap.

"What are you doing?" he asked.

Her gaze was on the barren hearth. "Waiting. Sooner or later Daisy or Miss Thorn will come in search of me."

Her faith was commendable. He leaned against the hearth. "I fear by that time the damage will be done."

She frowned, glancing up at him, lamplight shining in her dark eyes. "Damage?"

"To your reputation."

She drew herself up further. "You are a gentleman, sir."

He inclined his head. "Indeed I am. But the longer we are alone together, the quicker tongues will wag."

Her chin inched higher. "Let them wag. I have done nothing wrong, and I won't be pushed into apologizing."

There was that strength again. It called to him, beckoned him closer. He took a step without thinking.

The door rattled a moment before swinging open, and Miss Thorn strode into the room, eyes flashing like a sword. He'd once approached the woman for help with the idea that she and her cat were some sort of matchmakers. After all, the Duke of Wey, Sir Harold Orwell, Lord Worthington, and their host tonight, the Earl of Carrolton, had found brides through her. Now she looked like nothing so much as a winged Fury as she swept toward the sofa and held out one hand.

"Come, Ivy. Your sister is looking for you."

Ivy rose and hurried to her side. "Forgive me. The door jammed."

"Doors tend to do that when someone shoves a candelabra through the latches," she replied with a look in his direction.

He spread his hands. "May I remind you, madam, that I was trapped as well?"

"And may I remind you, sir, that I know your purpose for being in London."

Kendall stiffened. He hardly wanted it known he sought a marriage of convenience. That would attract all the wrong kinds of interest.

She put an arm around Ivy's waist as if determined to protect her. "You will call on me tomorrow, Lord Kendall, and we can discuss reparations."

Ivy pulled away from her. "Reparations? But nothing happened, Miss Thorn. I promise you."

"I believe you," the lady replied, look softening. "But others may not. Think of Daisy's reception if you will not think of your own." She nodded to Kendall. "Tomorrow, my lord. I am usually receiving by eleven. I expect you then, with an offer."

And she pulled her charge from the room before he could decide just who was manipulating whom.

Learn more at
www.reginascott.com/nevermarryamarquess

OTHER BOOKS BY REGINA SCOTT

FORTUNE'S BRIDES SERIES
Never Doubt a Duke
Never Borrow a Baronet
Never Envy an Earl
Never Vie for a Viscount

UNCOMMON COURTSHIPS SERIES
The Unflappable Miss Fairchild
The Incomparable Miss Compton
The Irredeemable Miss Renfield
The Unwilling Miss Watkin
An Uncommon Christmas

LADY EMILY CAPERS
Secrets and Sensibilities
Art and Artifice
Ballrooms and Blackmail
Eloquence and Espionage
Love and Larceny

MARVELOUS MUNROES SERIES
My True Love Gave to Me
Catch of the Season
The Marquis' Kiss
Sweeter Than Candy

SPY MATCHMAKER SERIES
The Husband Mission
The June Bride Conspiracy
The Heiress Objective

Perfection
And other books for Love Inspired Historical and
Timeless Regency collections.

ABOUT THE AUTHOR

R egina Scott started writing novels in the third grade. Thankfully for literature as we know it, she didn't sell her first novel until she learned a bit more about writing. Since her first book was published, her stories have traveled the globe, with translations in many languages including Dutch, German, Italian, and Portuguese. She now has more than forty-five published works of warm, witty romance.

She has never been a fan of boxing, though she learned to fence in college. Her husband, however, has a first-degree black belt in Judo and a fourth-degree black belt in Shudokan Karate. He helps her choreograph her fight scenes. Her critique partner and dear friend Kristy J. Manhattan, on the other hand, helped Regina come up with the idea for Fortune's Brides. Kristy is an avid fan of cats, supporting spay and neuter clinics and pet rescue groups. If Fortune resembles any cat you know, credit Kristy.

Regina Scott and her husband of 30 years reside in the Puget Sound area of Washington State on the way to Mt. Rainier. She has dressed as a Regency dandy, driven four-in-hand, and sailed on a tall ship, all in the name of research, of course. Learn more about her at her website at *www.reginascott.com.*

CPSIA information can be obtained
at www.ICGtesting.com
Printed in the USA
LVHW041449110619
620864LV00003B/554/P